BY THE JAGUAR:
TRANSFORMATION

CRISTINA RAYNE

http://CristinaRayneAuthor.blogspot.com

ISBN-10: 0692341560
ISBN-13: 978-0692341568

Dedicated to my sister, Rachel, who is one of my biggest fans

Also by Cristina Rayne

Elven King
Claimed by the Elven King
Claimed by the Elven Brothers: Decision (An Elven King Novella #1)
Claimed by the Elven Brothers: Fate (An Elven King Novella #2)
Shadows Beneath the Falling Snow (An Elven King Prequel Story)

Riverford Shifters
Tempted by the Jaguar #1: Transformation
Tempted by the Jaguar #2: Revelation
Tempted by the Jaguar #3: Ramification *coming soon

Erotic Tales from the Vampire Underground
Blood Escort: A Short Story

Urban and Epic Fantasy writing as C.G. Garcia

Fractured Multiverse
The Supreme Moment
Black Crimson (Blood Fire Chronicles Book 1) *coming soon

Old Souls Trilogy
Old Souls
The Ties That Bind the Soul
Old Souls Book 3 *coming soon

CHAPTER ONE

$\mathcal{K}$ylie Moore pulled her backpack from the backseat of her car and was in the process of straightening when she heard it, the soft scrape of a shoe slipping slightly on some loose gravel somewhere in the parking lot behind her. Freezing instinctually, she started to turn just as the back of her head was roughly pushed forward, and her temple slammed against the top of the doorframe. For one endless moment, it felt as though her entire skull had shattered as the inky blackness of the night exploded in a flash of white-hot pain across her vision.

Her backpack and keys fell from fingers gone slack from shock, and Kylie staggered back a step, blinded by pain and her mind a swirl of confusion. A sense of vertigo hit her as her world tilted sideways, only to feel the side of her body hit the pavement hard a second later.

A cry was torn from her lips as the sudden jolt caused what felt like a dozen knives to stab into her head. Then hands grabbed her arms and yanked them away from where she had been cradling her head, and her watery vision darkened almost completely in a sudden wash of pain as someone began dragging her along the asphalt away from her car, her body as limp and unresponsive as a ragdoll's.

Dazed thoughts of being carjacked melted into panicked, disjointed thoughts that, no, something much worse was happening, and Kylie tried to struggle. However, her consciousness was fading fast, and she just couldn't seem to make her body do *anything*.

Then her head banged into the edge of something hard…and the next thing Kylie knew, she found herself folded up into a very uncomfortable semblance of a fetal position, her hands stuck up behind her neck. She tried to flex her fingers, but both hands felt dead, as though she had been lying on them for quite some time.

It was pitch black, the air smelling heavily of motor oil and something rotten and sickly as though she was lying next to either a garbage can or a pile of vomit. The floor beneath her body vibrated, and a slight roaring filled her ears. Both the back of her head and one of her temples was throbbing something fierce, and she couldn't help the small moan that fell from her lips.

What the hell was going on? Her head pounding, confusion, her mouth dry—it was as if she had just woken up in the weirdest place ever with the worst hangover in existence. Only, she didn't drink.

Kylie tried to move both her arms and legs, trying to remember what she had been doing. She'd had a study group for genetics class today. She was sure she had left the university library; she could remember getting into her car and driving off towards the freeway with the intention of going back to her apartment. Then…then…

Something rough and sturdy painfully dug into her bare ankles and upper thighs simultaneously as she tried to straighten her legs, and her wrists met that same barrier as she tried to bring her arms down from her head. It was only then that the fogginess of her mind suddenly evaporated into terror. She was freaking *tied up*!

Now in a panic, Kylie yanked her wrists hard against what she now knew to be coils of rope and nearly choked as the sharp movement caused an unnoticed cord of rope to tighten around her neck.

Rather than just tied together, a length of rope had also been connected to the bindings around her wrists and then wrapped around her neck, insuring that any pulling on her part would only lead to strangling herself.

She frantically thrashed her body around in an effort to free her legs, but the thick rope cut painfully into her skin and only seemed to tighten. Whoever had tied her up had done their job extremely well.

In some remote part of her mind not yet touched by hysteria, Kylie desperately hoped that this was just some cruel, horribly misguided prank someone was playing on her while the more practical part of her brain was screaming that she was in shit so deep she was already drowning. Someone *had* to have hit her over the head. Her temple throbbed too sharply to attribute it to even a migraine.

A memory surfaced, one she wished she didn't know. For the past year, half a dozen women had gone missing from various places within the city, even a freshman from her own university. No bodies, no clues from security footage or witnesses, *nothing* was ever found of them again, as though they had all literally vanished from the face of the earth. The last one had vanished a couple of months ago.

No—not a couple of months, today *if I don't figure out how to get the hell out of here!*

Kylie managed to roll her body to the left, but immediately hit a barrier. After a bit of a struggle, she succeeded in rolling herself in the other direction only to immediately roll onto what felt like a shovel. She froze even though the metal edge was digging uncomfortably into her shoulders, on the verge of a full-on panic attack. The vibrating floor and the smells now made horrifying sense. She was in the freaking trunk of a car!

She began to struggle and strain against her bindings with a frenzied effort, nearly biting through her tongue in an attempt to keep the anguished wails of terror at bay. It was obvious she had been knocked out at some point, and even though her mouth had not been covered, there was no way she was about to possibly alert her abductor that she was now awake.

They were probably driving on a freeway or highway, so there was little to no chance that anyone would be able to hear her screaming above the normal rumble of travel and passing cars. She had no idea how long she had even been unconscious. Her only chance would be to either free herself before the monster, or monsters, opened the trunk, or if failing that, screaming her lungs out when the car stopped.

Her wrists burned as she strained, but her abductor had left almost no wiggle room. The ropes might as well have been zip ties for all the progress she had made. By now her hands were so dead she couldn't even wiggle her fingers, and her legs were screaming with pain.

It was no use.

Kylie fell limp and clenched her jaw against the sob of despair that wanted to break loose. There was a very good chance that she was about to die that day, and damned if she was going to give the bastard the satisfaction of seeing her tears, the fear that was threatening to choke the breath from her. She had to save her strength, keep her mind as clear as her throbbing headache allowed, her eyes sharp. She took a long, shuddering breath, trying not to gag on the smells that were coming from the trunk's carpet, trying to calm the pounding of her heart that sounded as loud as gunfire in her ears.

By the time the car started to slow down, Kylie felt as though she had been trapped in that trunk for days. She had debated back and forth on whether or not to pretend to still be unconscious or to try screaming the moment the car stopped, and now that the moment of truth was almost here, Kylie's panic returned with a vengeance. What if she screamed and that was the thing that doomed her? What if she kept her eyes closed, pretended to still be unconscious, and she missed seeing the only chance to escape she would get?

The moment the car came to a complete stop, something in Kylie snapped, and she was screaming for help before she even realized that she was going to do it. Bellowing at the top of her lungs, she managed a dozen "help me's" before the trunk was wrenched open and three more after before a large, dark figure abruptly filled her vision. An equally large, sweaty and calloused hand roughly slapped over her mouth mid-scream.

Kylie instinctually tried to bite at the hand. However, it lifted before she could really sink her teeth into anything, and a second later her mouth exploded with pain as that same hand backhanded her with brutal force before she could even think to scream again. She felt the soft tissue of her bottom lip slice across the sharp edges of her teeth, and a trickle of hot blood began to flow into her mouth.

She only had just enough time to suck in a shocked breath before she was wrenched out of the trunk by her shoulders and promptly dumped face-first onto the ground into a cluster of tall weeds, jarring her head and causing pain like a knife stabbing into her skull to shoot through her temple. Kylie gritted her teeth and immediately forced her body to roll onto its side.

"Somebody! *Help me!*" she screamed over and

over as soon as her face was free of the weeds even though the only things she could see were darkness and the dark silhouette of dozens of trees.

It was hopeless. Now that she had seen the trees and knew that he had brought her into the forest that surrounded Riverford, a forest that went on for miles in all directions, it was pretty much game over for her. Yet, she just couldn't make herself stop crying out for help. She couldn't give up on the slim hope that someone else just might be nearby, just might be able to hear her screams, because dammit! She couldn't die now! She couldn't die without ever knowing what had happened to her parents! Hadn't fate shit on Paul and her enough!

So Kylie screamed and screamed and writhed within her bindings, probably doing terrible damage to her legs and wrists as she strained to break the ropes, but not even her anger and desperation was enough to free her. It was only after she had screamed her voice to almost nonexistence that she realized that her abductor was standing only a foot away from her head, just—standing there with his head down, watching her futile struggles.

There was no moon that night, so even her dark-adjusted eyes couldn't make out more than the outline of his body. He was tall, looming over her still and quiet like one of the phantom trees surrounding them. Was he smiling? Smirking? Or worse, did he have no expression at all? The thought of her possibly giving him exactly the show that he wanted made Kylie immediately stop her thrashing.

For the space of what felt like an eternity, the only sound was the rustle of the wind flowing through the multitudes of tree branches and her ragged breathing. That he hadn't said one word to her was more terrifying than if he had been reciting a list of horrible things he was about to do to her.

Kylie told herself she wouldn't scream, that she wouldn't move until she saw an opening. Tied up the way she was, he had only left her two possible weapons. Now that one of them, her voice, had obviously failed to bring her help, she had only one possible, one very *sharp* way out of this as her cut lip and the taste of blood in her mouth could attest. He only had to get close to her, or more specifically his *neck*, in just the right position. One tiny hope; one try.

She had to wait; she had to stay sharp. Kylie could almost hear her father whispering those words to her again, words that she had lived by, that she had clung to as her anchor for the past twelve years.

However, when he sank down onto one knee and she saw the large pair of metal scissors moving towards her stomach, Kylie couldn't help flinching with a small cry of alarm. Her abductor's free hand shot out of the darkness to wrap around her neck, squeezing with just enough pressure for her to feel the rope coiled around her neck begin to bite into her delicate flesh but not enough to strangle. A warning.

He was now close enough to her that she could see the whites of his eyes, could see him staring directly at her with unblinking dark eyes that sent a shiver up her spine. There was nothing human in that gaze, nothing even remotely resembling an emotion. Just what kind of monster was she at the mercy of?

Without moving his gaze from her face, he began to slowly cut away at the hem of her blouse. Kylie lay frozen on her side, afraid to move, afraid to even breathe as she felt the cold metal of the scissors brush against her skin as they slowly moved up her abdomen.

It was in those dead eyes. She could see it as plainly as if he had announced it. He would not be satisfied with just cutting all her clothes off. He wouldn't be satisfied because he had never intended to violate her body in the way she had feared. No, this was a monster the likes of which she could have never imagined.

Kylie could feel a scream welling up in her throat. In a second or two it would break free and with it, very likely her sanity. Kylie opened her mouth, and a sound emerged that she had never heard come from a human throat, a long, drawn-out keening of pure despair that seemed to come directly from her soul.

...and something deep within her entire being shattered.

CHAPTER TWO

A wave of what felt like the biggest muscle spasm she had ever had washed through Kylie's entire body a split-second before every inch of her began to contract and expand as though she was a balloon being inflated to the brink of bursting. For a painful beat, the ropes around her wrists, neck, ankles, and thighs cut excruciatingly into her flesh before inexplicably snapping as though they were made of straw. Her strange keening also began to change in pitch, to expand until the roar of an apex predator filled the once eerily silent night.

Rage, fear, and a sense of blood lust filled her mind. An enemy was here! An enemy was hurting her! With a deafening roar, Kylie lunged at the figure that had fallen back onto his ass, that was frantically trying to scoot away from her. She could now see him as clearly as though it were twilight. She felt huge; she felt powerful as two large paws of golden, black-spotted fur slammed onto his chest, claws sinking past layers of cloth that felt as flimsy as silk and tearing into that soft, soft flesh as her enemy was flattened to the ground with a shriek of pain.

The coppery smell of blood and another acrid scent of something she had never smelled before filled her nostrils, and the rage that saturated her every pore instantly doubled until all she could think about, all she wanted was the taste of that blood on her tongue. She opened her jaws wide and went for her attacker's throat just as what felt like a battering ram hit her squarely on the side, causing Kylie to tumble uncontrollably off the bleeding body until she landed in a heap onto her side.

With a roar, she scrambled onto all fours, hunching low into a defensive stance and her tail lashing sharply like the crack of a whip behind her. Her mind was so lost to the rage, to the fear of being attacked that she didn't even stop to wonder why she was on all fours, that she roared, or that she actually had a *tail* to lash behind her. Her entire world had narrowed down to the large spotted feline standing challengingly between her and her prey that was currently staggering off into the protection of the trees, its eyes flashing with a bit of night shine as it stared her down but did not try to move closer.

Kylie lashed out at the much larger great cat, swatting at the air between them warningly with her claws, before backing up a couple of steps and resuming her defensive stance with a series of sharp chuffs. That was *her* prey! How dare the other, one of her own *brethren*, try to take it from her!

She let out another angry chuff and clawed the ground. The other cat blinked its large eyes and then tilted its head in a manner that her senses were screaming was utterly *wrong*—unnatural.

Slowly it sat back onto its haunches and then before her alarmed eyes, the spotted cat's entire body began to ripple in an utterly unsettling way before the mass of its body began to shrink down and rearrange itself. Spotted fur rapidly melted into smooth, human skin until everything settled and the body of a man crouched in its place.

Her mind in its current state just could not comprehend what it had just seen. A naked, black-haired man now crouched before her, but he still smelled the same. He still smelled like the great cat of before.

The man stared back at her warily, moving to sit with his knees bent up, and then he carefully rested his arms onto them.

"It's all right," he said softly in a deep, nonthreatening voice. "Be calm. Be calm. I'm not angry. I'm not going to hurt you."

Kylie snarled at him and took a cautious step back. What was he saying? He attacked her! He let her prey escape!

"You're okay," he cooed in that same, soft voice. "There's no danger here. I just want to help you. Will you let me help you?"

Help her? Some of her rage subsided as utter confusion began to creep into her mind. What had just happened here?

"Can you shift back now? So we can talk?" the man asked, his eyes wide and imploring.

Kylie paused in the process of baring her teeth, the word "shift" tickling the edges of a distant memory even as a surge of fear washed over her, effectively snuffing out the uncontrollable rage of before. It was *him*, she realized suddenly, this stranger who had turned from cat to man before her very eyes. It was him she was afraid of, afraid that he was going to find out about—

—that I'm a—

Her eyes flickered down to the ground, to her two spotted paws with claws fully extended and the fur matted with blood, and she abruptly let out a sound of dismay that did not at all sound like something that should have come out of any kind of feline's throat.

Shit! I'm a jaguar! Kylie suddenly screeched in utter shock within her mind, a mind that was now once again completely her own. She scrambled back in a panic until her rump hit a tree, looking with horror at the unknown naked man who had suddenly jumped to his feet.

He saw! He saw!

"No—don't—!" he exclaimed, taking a step towards her, but she didn't wait to hear the rest.

Kylie bounded off into the night, running as though the Devil, himself, was on her heels, dodging trees and brush and jumping over exposed roots with an almost preternatural grace even as her mind was in full-blown freak-out mode. She had *shifted*! Another shifter had *seen* her! How had this happened?

Like a mantra, those thoughts ran through her mind over and over as she raced through the dense forest with no destination in mind except *away*. She ran as fast as she could even though she couldn't tell if he was following her, couldn't tell if his scent was among the thousand different scents that she drew in as she panted. The assault of unknown smells almost overwhelmed her, fueled her fear and panic, and Kylie had no idea how to separate herself from it.

So she just ran until she could hear the hum of

various vehicles zooming down what she hoped was the east highway out of Riverford and could see the faint flashes of their headlights through the trees as they drove past. By now, her breathing had become severely labored, and various muscles were beginning to scream with pain in places she was not used to.

She slowed down to a more manageable pace and turned west to run parallel to the road but still well hidden by the trees and the darkness. *I have to get home! I have to call Paul!*

Never mind that she had been attacked and abducted by what was probably a serial killer or that she had been seconds away from ripping out his throat. The only thing that mattered now, that *could* matter, was that she had *shifted* and had been seen by another shifter.

She had to get to Paul. He was the only chance she had now.

CHAPTER THREE

Kylie dashed across the highway and back into the cover of the forest, making it across before any more cars managed to come around the bend. The way her heart pounded within the chest of her new form felt utterly unfamiliar and scary, but she knew now was not the time to freak out about it. She had no way of knowing if she had managed to lose the black-haired man back there in the forest, or if he had even decided to give chase in the first place. She would have plenty of time to fall apart once she made it back to the relative safety of her apartment.

This area was thankfully familiar. The road was definitely the east highway out of Riverford. She moved through the trees as fast as her waning strength could sustain, heading north along the perimeter of the city towards a children's neighborhood park that skated along the edges of the forest. It was only a few blocks from her apartment complex.

It was still the dead of night, so hopefully no one would be out to see the large jaguar moving through the shadows. Being shot by a frightened neighbor on top of everything else she had already endured that night would just be the rotten cherry on top of a sundae gone sour.

By the time she reached the park, Kylie's entire body trembled with exhaustion. She was unable to even prevent her tongue from hanging out of her mouth as she panted. Her bones also ached in a strange way that made her feel as though she had injured them somehow and they were dangerously on the verge of shattering. Even so, she only paused long enough behind one of the trees along the edge to take in a few deep, wheezing breaths while her eyes swept the length of the park within her field of vision, looking for any signs of movement among all the swing sets, slides, and jungle gyms.

Only when she was satisfied that section of the park was empty did Kylie shoot out from the cover of the trees as though she had been fired from a cannon and raced across the grass to the street and the first apartment building to the right. Keeping to the shadows, she slunk along the building to an alleyway that she hoped would offer her more protection than moving through the residential streets.

As Kylie bounded down the alley, her once sharp vision began to blur, and she could no longer see the far end of the dark alley as clearly. Then something that felt like the worst muscle spasm she had ever had rolled across her entire body, starting from her shoulder to the tip of her tail, causing her to stumble and fall onto her belly just when she emerged from the alley into the street.

For one, panic-filled moment, Kylie couldn't get up, all four limbs shaking as though she was starting to seize. Shit! Was she starting to shift back?

"Whoa! What the hell!" a young male voice suddenly yelped, causing Kylie to instinctually turn her head and snarl in the direction of the voice.

A surge of adrenaline shot through her veins, and Kylie was instantly back on all fours before she had even made the decision to move, crouching defensively as a pair of teenaged boys stood frozen along the curb of the street a mere five feet away. That same acrid scent she had smelled after she had attacked her abductor back in the forest filled the air, and it was then that Kylie understood what it was she smelled.

Fear. Pungent and sharp and exciting, it was not a sweet scent, or even a meaty, organic scent. The scent of fear did not even remotely resemble anything she had ever smelled as a human. The aroma was almost an emotion, one that the feline part of her understood *very* well.

It was then that the urge to lunge at the two boys nearly overwhelmed her, and only the small part of her that was still completely human, the part that realized the horror of what she was on the brink of doing, managed to turn her body just as she started to pounce on the nearest boy who had suddenly become prey and sprang off in the opposite direction instead. With her own fear and disgust spurring her on, Kylie ran down the street with a renewed vigor, her control hanging by a thread.

She had to get home. She had to get home before she accidentally ran into someone else because she wasn't so sure she would have the strength of mind to run away a second time. That fear drove her down street after street at a speed she should not have been capable of as exhausted as she was, a large shadow just a bit lighter than the surrounding night that could very easily be mistaken for a large dog to anyone who may have caught a glimpse of her.

At the first sight of her apartment building, Kylie couldn't help the whine of relief that burst out from deep within her throat. Her vision was already losing its feline acuity, and the strange spasms of before were once again spreading across her body. She made it a few feet across the parking lot before her body simply collapsed mid-lope. She fell onto her side, and her body began to violently seize, causing her to accidentally bite down hard on her lolling tongue. The salty, coppery taste of blood filled her mouth as she felt various parts of her body tighten, then stretch until she felt as though her muscles were about to tear.

Kylie opened her mouth to roar, but a very human cry of pain shattered the silence instead. Startled, she opened tear-filled eyes and saw her once again human hand, her fingers stained dark, lying on the asphalt near her face. She shuddered, with both the chill of the night air and the lingering spasms that still rocked her body and drew in an equally shaky breath. However, when she tried to lift her head, a wave of utter exhaustion washed through her body so powerfully, so heavy, that for a few terrifying moments, it was almost too much effort to breathe.

Fighting off panic, Kylie forced herself to relax completely and concentrate on merely breathing, trying not to think of the utter mortification she would feel if she passed out right then and there and someone stumbled upon her naked, unconscious body in the morning. However, instead of going away, her exhaustion only seemed to be getting worse and her eyelids heavier, and Kylie realized being found naked was exactly what was about to happen if she didn't somehow manage to drag her butt over to her parking space where she prayed to everything holy her car, and more importantly her backpack with her key to the apartment, would be. She still only had vague memories of her head being bashed against the doorframe of her car, but she wasn't altogether sure it had happened here in this parking lot.

She gritted her teeth and forced herself to roll over onto her stomach. Then drawing a deep, steadying breath, she managed to climb onto her knees even though it felt as if someone had dropped a hundred pound weight onto her back. How ironic that she was now forced to move on all fours while in her human form.

It was slow going, but Kylie finally made it to the end of the lot without incident and literally felt tears well up in her eyes when she saw her little black sedan parked next to her neighbors' SUV. At least now she knew where she had been attacked.

Thoughts of her attacker, of the pain of the rope cutting deeply into her flesh suddenly flooded her mind, and Kylie viciously cut off that line of thinking.

She couldn't handle any of that right now. She would fall apart, and she could *not* allow that to happen again, especially out in the open like this. Losing it had already caused her to involuntarily shift. What if it happened again and some of her neighbors happened to stumble on her?

Maybe the universe finally decided to take pity on her because as Kylie dragged herself between the two vehicles, her eyes immediately caught sight of her keys just a little ways beneath her car. She had been afraid that they had been lost somewhere in the trunk from hell she had awakened in, and seeing them there lifted just a little bit of the enormous weight on her back, enough that she was able to force herself upright onto her knees on the first try.

Please let it be there...

Kylie tugged on the handle of the rear driver's side door and found it unlocked. On the floorboard was the item she sought. Leaning farther into the car, she grabbed her backpack and unzipped the small pouch in the front. Pulling out her cell phone was like finding the prize after running a marathon.

She could finally call Paul. He would know what to do.

Her windows were tinted pretty dark. It would probably be okay for her to hunker down in the backseat of her car for the twenty or thirty minutes it would take him to drive to her apartment because she really didn't think she had the strength to make it to her door, even though her apartment was on the first floor.

Using the last dregs of her strength, she thrust herself onto the backseat in a sort of dive, pulling the door closed after she had wiggled around and was situated. Just that simple exertion caused her head to swim and her breathing to become as labored as though she had been running for hours. Her energy reserves were nearly completely depleted. How long before her body just said "screw it" and just shut down? Skipping dinner today was seriously coming back to bite her in the ass.

Kylie took a couple of deep, calming breaths and quickly turned her phone on to call Paul. After the fourth ring, a bit of panic began to surface. Had he forgotten his cell phone in his office again? Like her, he did not have a landline, his reasoning being that he was seldom home. If she managed to survive this horrendous night, then maybe they should both rethink the matter.

On the fifth ring, the phone went to his voice mail, and Kylie hung up with a curse. Leaving him a message was absolutely out of the question. She slowly turned towards the apartment building with a look of despair. She wasn't sure she could make it to the building, much less her apartment. She looked down at her phone. Did she dare call one of her friends? But—how in the hell would she even begin to explain what she was doing sitting in her backseat naked and seconds away from passing out.

No. No one except Paul could know *anything* had happened to her at all. It was too dangerous. It was also too dangerous to stay in the car. If she passed out and someone found her before she managed to get a hold of Paul...

Her phone's ringtone suddenly went off, nearly scaring her half to death, the sudden adrenaline surge making her chest constrict painfully. For a couple of seconds, Kylie had to fight off the blackness that had begun to enter the edges of her vision before she was able to clumsily tap the "talk" button on her phone and bring it up to her ear. For a split-second, she had a momentary panic when she realized that she had answered before checking to see who was calling, but then a familiar deep voice said her name anxiously, and relief like she had never felt washed through her like a balm.

"Paul..." she said, her voice cracking as she very nearly lost her hard-fought battle against her threatening tears.

"What happened? Are you hurt?" Paul demanded, fear making his voice sound deeper than normal.

"I can't—can you please come to my apartment?" Kylie pleaded, hating how young and pathetic she sounded. Now was not the time to fall apart, dammit! "Too much has happened. Just please come."

"Kylie…" Paul replied, sounding anguished. "I'm not in Riverford. I'm in Dallas for the conference, remember?"

Her heart instantly sank. She *had* forgotten. Kylie glanced at the clock on her phone. Ten after five. It was much later in the morning than she had thought. Even by plane, he was at least a little over an hour away. It would take a miracle for him to reach her in less than two, and by then, probably three-fourths of her apartment complex would be heading to the parking lot for work or school. There was no way she wouldn't be seen before Paul could get to her.

"Paul—I *shifted*," Kylie told him urgently.

She could practically hear his shock in the sudden silence on the other end. "Did someone see you?" he demanded, the fear even more blatant in his tone.

"Yes," she admitted in a small voice.

"Another shifter or a human?"

"Both."

"Where are you now?"

"I'm in my car in the parking lot of my apartment building."

"Why are you still—no there's no time. Listen to me, Kylie. Get inside your apartment, and turn your phone off. Don't call *anyone*. Don't answer the door unless you hear me say the secret word. I would tell you to destroy your phone, but not having one would be worse. I'll be there as soon as humanly possible."

Kylie glanced out the window and zeroed in on the faraway door of her apartment that was, at the most, the length of a football field away but might as well have been miles. Why oh why did she have to live in a complex where the parking was all the way in the back for everyone?

Nevertheless—there were no if ands or buts about it. She would just have to make it on her own. Paul was on his way. She would have to draw strength from that thought alone.

"I'll be waiting," she said with as much determination as she could muster before hanging up immediately, sure she would start crying if she heard his voice again.

There was no use adding to his worries just yet. Kylie had a feeling everything would come crashing down soon enough.

Kylie wasn't sure how, but after at least thirty minutes of alternating between short spurts of dragging herself and pausing to fight off the darkness that was threatening to overwhelm her mind, the door to her apartment was finally before her. She let out a sound that was half-sob, half-laugh. For one terrifying moment, she had very nearly teetered over the knife-thin ledge she had been moving along into unconsciousness halfway there, but by some miracle, she had managed to hold onto consciousness by the skin of her teeth.

The level of exhaustion that she was currently feeling was unlike anything she had ever experienced. She was sure that she had just scraped her knees and elbows raw, but she was so tired that the only thing she could feel was a bone-deep numbness. By sheer force of will, Kylie forced herself to her knees and leaned against the door as she struggled to slide the key into the lock.

After what felt like an eternity of fumbling, she finally managed to get the door open and promptly fell across the threshold with a weak grunt as she landed face-first onto the carpet of her living room. The world was quickly fading fast, but Kylie shook her head in an effort to clear the haziness that had started to creep in and struggled to pull herself the rest of the way inside.

Her hand moved on autopilot to close the door, and her last thought before her mind lost the battle with consciousness was that she hadn't locked the door.

CHAPTER FOUR

L oud pounding sounded right next to her ear, and Kylie's eyes flew open, her heart practically tearing out of her chest. It took a couple of seconds before the room blurred into focus, and with some confusion, she realized that she was lying down on the carpet near the front door.

What in the—

A series of rapid, loud raps on the front door made her jump a second time, and Kylie scrambled onto her knees, nearly face-planting on the floor when the world suddenly did a one-eighty. She squeezed her eyes closed with a groan and grabbed her head between her hands, the unexpected vertigo making her feel queasy. It was then, her head bent down as she slowly opened her eyes again, that she noticed that she didn't have a stitch on.

"Shit!" Kylie cried as she scrambled unsteadily onto her feet, memories of last night's horrors finally beginning to rise out of the confusion of her still sleep-fogged mind.

That was probably Paul at the door!

Kylie started to turn, intent on going to her bedroom to throw on some clothes, when she froze. No—it couldn't be Paul. She hadn't heard him say it. The secret word.

She only had time to take an alarmed step back before the knob started to turn. Shit! The door wasn't locked!

Kylie dashed forward and slammed both hands against the door as hard as she could just as it started to open. However, the door was pushed heavily from the other side, and whoever was standing there managed to wedge a white-sneakered foot into the crack that had momentarily opened. With a cry of terror, she shoved at the door with all her might, but it was as though she was trying to move a brick wall for all the door budged.

"I just want to talk," a vaguely familiar male voice said, sounding much too calm given the battle of force they were engaged in.

"You have the wrong apartment!" Kylie said through gritted teeth. She was still feeling incredibly weak from her ordeal last night and could feel that she was just seconds away from losing the battle.

The guy snorted. "We both know that isn't true," he said, sounding rather matter-of-fact. "I can *smell* you."

His odd words gave her pause only for a split-second, but it was the edge he needed to finally push the door open wide enough for him to squeeze through. In a panic, rather than make a break for her bedroom, Kylie grabbed the doorknob and pulled the door flush against her front and scrambled back until her back hit the wall, using the door to cover her nudity.

Immediately she felt a tug on the door, and Kylie gripped the doorknob so tightly that her entire hand was beginning to hurt. "No! Don't!" she moaned desperately.

The stranger abruptly stopped trying to pull the door away from her.

"I'm not going to hurt you," he said softly.

Kylie sucked in a sharp breath. Those words, that tone—she had heard them before, just last night, in fact. It was *him*, the shifter guy, the jaguar. How in the hell had he found her?

"I can smell you."

She mentally cursed as his earlier words echoed mockingly within her mind, remembering how acute her sense of smell had been while she had been in her shifted form. He had tracked her. She had never had any chance of escaping him at all.

"I—" Kylie had no idea what to do. She was quite literally backed into a corner, and her options were practically nil. Weak and trembling behind a door, she doubted she could solve her nudity problem by shifting since she both lacked the energy and more importantly, had no idea how to initiate the change in the first place.

Light was pouring through the window beside her, too much for it to still be early morning. Surely she had been passed out for longer than a couple of hours, so where was Paul? Had his plane been delayed?

She needed to stall for time, and that meant getting him talking and playing dumb.

"I—don't have any clothes on," Kylie admitted.

She was completely unprepared for his sudden laugh. "Why didn't you say so in the first place?" he scolded.

Kylie couldn't help feeling slightly offended by his tone. "Maybe it was because I was too busy trying to keep some psycho from breaking into my apartment!" she snapped.

"The door was unlocked," he said pointedly, sounding completely unrepentant.

"And?" she shot back hostilely. "Since when does that give every asshole on the street permission to waltz into the apartment of someone they don't know?"

"You're certainly taking all of this a lot better than I'd thought you would," he remarked. She could hear the sound of cloth rustling as he talked. "Things may be more serious than I thought."

Suddenly he thrust something dark between the door and the wall. Kylie shrank away instinctually before she saw that it was a thin, navy blue sweater.

"Put that on, and come out. As I said before, for now I only want to talk."

The sweater was utterly saturated with the smell of him, of something earthy and powerful that she knew she would have never smelled yesterday. The jaguar's senses were muted but very much still a part of her even in her human form.

Her nostrils instinctually flared as she slipped his sweater over her head, his scent starting to make her head spin. She got the feeling that by putting on his sweater, she had just done something that she really shouldn't have done, but between some vague feelings of misgivings and parading out naked in front of some unknown guy, there really was no competition.

Kylie was relieved to discover that the sweater

was more than long enough to cover her ass. After pushing the overly-long sleeves up past her wrists, she hesitantly slipped out from behind the door. She half-expected to be met with the sight of a bare-chested man, but the dark-haired man standing only a foot or two away from the door—and completely blocking that potential escape route—was dressed properly in a simple white t-shirt and jeans.

It had been dark back in the forest, and she most definitely had not been herself, so Kylie really didn't remember much about the shifter that had confronted her. Now, she couldn't help but stare as she noted his tanned, well-muscled arms and not just for the obvious reasons. Either he had not been trying too hard to push open the door earlier or shifting had changed her body even in its human form. She wasn't sure which idea disturbed her more.

Her gaze rose to his face, and Kylie could feel her entire body stiffen as she fought to control her startlement. To say that the guy was hot didn't even begin to accurately describe him. He had the type of chiseled, perfectly proportioned face with plump, luscious lips and just the right amount of stubble on his cheeks and chin to give him that sexy edge that photographers or painters wept over. His eyes, a hazel color more golden than brown regarded her with all the wariness of a predator presented with an unknown entity.

Kylie was grateful for that look. It instantly dragged her mind out of the gutter it had fast descended into and back to the seriousness of the situation. Her eyes flickered once towards the door to her bedroom. It had a lock, and the window was large enough for her to climb out. Could she make it?

A slight narrowing of her uninvited visitor's eyes was all the answer she needed. The last thing she wanted was to end up tackled on the ground while wearing only an overlarge sweater.

"Okay. Let's talk," she said, gesturing over to the couch.

The smile he flashed her made her heart seize, and now completely irritated with herself, Kylie tore her eyes away from his mouth and stomped over to the couch while the door clicked shut behind her. What was wrong with her anyway? She was beginning to wonder if last night's horrors had robbed her of her sanity after all.

She gave her head a mental shake. Now was not the time to think about her kidnapping. She needed her mind sharp and her emotions stable to safely maneuver the potential minefield this jaguar shifter presented.

Kylie sat on the far end of the couch, making sure his sweater adequately covered all her naughty bits. She watched him approach, all feline grace even as a human. She was relieved when he sat at the other end of the couch, respecting her personal space.

"So, will you at least tell me your name?" she asked, hating how stiff her words sounded. This was not a man she could afford to show any weakness to, no matter the circumstances.

"Hunter Rivera." He raised an eyebrow expectantly.

She hesitated, but then realized that by knowing her address, finding out her name was only a Google search away.

"Kylie Moore." Then before he could say anything else, she asked, "Do you want to tell me why you think you're entitled to forcing your way into my apartment? Why I should even *talk* to you instead of calling the cops?"

Hunter's eyes suddenly hardened. "Take a good look at your hands," he said quietly. "That's all the permission I need, given it was *you* that entered *my* territory and did what you did."

Wondering if he was trying to trick her in some way, Kylie was reluctant to take her eyes off him, so she raised her hands to eye level instead. She immediately gasped in shock when she realized that her hands were splattered with dried blood. Without a word, she abruptly rose and headed towards her bathroom.

She had already turned on the tap in the sink when Hunter's large form filled the doorway. He stood there silently and watched with no discernable expression as she vigorously soaped and scrubbed her hands raw until even the blood beneath her fingernails had been cleansed. By then, Kylie's entire body was shaking with the effort of trying to keep it together, and her breathing sounded sharp and panicky. But damned if she was going to fall apart in front of this man without knowing his intentions.

"He's alive you know," Hunter said suddenly, making her jump.

Slowly, she turned to look at him. That wary look had entered his eyes again.

"Although you damned near gutted him, he managed to get back to his car and drive to the outskirts of the city before crashing into an auto repair shop."

Kylie turned her head and looked down at her reddened, damp hands. "He was going to hurt me," she whispered.

She could see him nod out of the corner of her eye. "I was hunting nearby," Hunter said. "I heard you screaming."

"He snuck up behind me when I was reaching into my backseat for my backpack," she continued, the words suddenly tumbling from her lips as if of their own accord. "He knocked me out, and I woke up tied up inside his trunk. He took me into the forest. He had scissors. He started to—started to—c-cut—" Kylie wrapped her trembling arms around her waist and squeezed tightly. "Then I—I—"

"Hey, it's okay," Hunter said gently, reaching a hand out to her, but stopping just short of touching her shoulder. "For now, why don't you go change. I'll be waiting for you in the living room."

Without waiting for a response, he turned and left her to try to regain her composure.

CHAPTER FIVE

When Kylie walked back into the living room more than half an hour later, now dressed in jeans and a simple long-sleeved shirt, Hunter was seated back on the couch staring pensively at the various picture frames of family and friends that hung on the wall next to the TV. Frankly, she was surprised that he had not barged into her bedroom to drag her out.

She didn't know what to make of him. It was clear that he wasn't going to leave until he received whatever answers he had tracked her down for. For that reason alone, she wasn't quite ready to trust in his professions of not hurting her. Just because he hadn't hurt her *yet* didn't mean he wouldn't later if he felt her answers were less than satisfactory.

Once her trembling had more or less stopped,

Kylie had shut herself into her room and quickly threw on the first set of clothes that had caught her eye in her closet. She had even put on a pair of her running shoes, seriously contemplating trying to escape through the window. However, her phone was likely still on the floor somewhere near the front door, and she had never memorized Paul's number. Even if she holed up at a friend's place, Hunter would likely literally sniff her out before Paul could find her.

She was screwed either way, so the best thing she could do was cooperate with Hunter until Paul showed up. At the very least, Paul would add an unexpected variable to the mix, and maybe, just maybe she and Paul would be able to talk their way out of this whole nightmare without raising anyone's suspicions.

It was now almost five hours since she had made it inside her apartment and collapsed in front of the door. Either Paul had been unable to catch a flight home on such short notice and was forced to drive or his flight was delayed. Whichever it was, it probably wouldn't be long before he arrived. She only had to hold it together for a little while longer…feign ignorance…

"What are you thinking?" Hunter suddenly asked, startling Kylie from her thoughts.

She turned her gaze back to him but didn't move closer to the couch, nervously bunching the sweater she had planned to return to him between her hands.

"This is a nightmare," she replied. "That's what I'm thinking. People don't turn into freaking leopards, no matter how scared they are."

He scowled. "Jaguars, not leopards," he corrected, an edge to his voice that made her think that particular mistake was made often, though in her case, she had made it purposely. She knew damn well there were only four different cat shifter clans in Riverford, and none of them were leopards. "But you're right. *Humans* don't turn into animals, but *shifters* do."

"*Shifters?*" she echoed with feigned confusion.

"As in shape-shifters." He was watching her face very closely. "Or were-jaguars if that helps you understand it better."

"Were-jaguars…you mean, like *werewolves?*" Kylie exclaimed as incredulously as she could manage. "But—but—last night there wasn't—"

Hunter sighed. "You really don't know anything about this, do you? We don't shift at the full moon if that's what you're thinking."

"How can you be so calm about all of this?" she demanded. "I turned into a freaking jaguar! I nearly *killed* someone, no matter that the sick bastard deserved it! How can any of this be *real*?"

He held up his hands. "Fair enough. Come and sit down. I obviously can't take you to see the Elders when you're this confused. We need to figure out a few things first."

Kylie stayed rooted to her spot. "Elders? What do you mean *elders*? I'm not going *anywhere* with you!"

"No, not yet," he agreed, "but Kylie, let me make something clear right now. You are a shifter, and as such, you are expected to obey certain laws. If it had only been me that witnessed your shift last night, then the situation would not be as dire as it is."

Kylie shrank back in true alarm. "What do you mean?"

"You shifted in front of a human not in the know," he explained, "and that is the one law that must never be broken."

"But I didn't know I could even...!" she protested.

He nodded. "And now that I know that, we can fix this, figure out what happened here."

After staring each other down for a long, tense moment, Kylie finally set his crumpled sweater on the arm of the couch before she cautiously seated herself as far away from him as she could.

"You were adopted weren't you?" Hunter asked.

Her eyes widened. "How could you possibly

know that?"

"Because that's the only explanation that would make sense here," he said wryly. "If your parents had been shifters, then there's no way you wouldn't have known about your own heritage, not even if you were a Deadend."

Kylie went positively rigid; she simply couldn't help it.

"What's a 'dead end'?" she asked.

Just saying the word left a very bad taste in her mouth. She damn well knew what it meant and had hoped that she would never hear it spoken again for as long as she lived. However, she didn't want to raise his suspicions by not asking the obvious question.

Hunter's lips twisted in what looked like disgust. "It's what kids born to shifter parents are called when they lack the ability to shift. It happens very rarely, but until recently, it was seen as something shameful—a weakness in a shifter family's bloodline or for other, equally stupid reasons. These children were almost always sent to live with humans from the moment their inability to shift was discovered."

"I see," Kylie said frostily. "You think my birth parents abandoned me?"

"Maybe," he replied reluctantly, "or they might have been killed. Lord knows we jaguars have our share of enemies. How you came to be raised by humans could have been for any number of reasons. Some parents are reluctant to give up a Deadend child but do not wish them to grow up with this stigma. Thus, adoption is seen as the best option for the kid."

"But I shifted," she pointed out.

"The fact of which muddies the waters completely. How old were you when you were adopted?"

"Just a baby. Why?"

"And you know *nothing* about your birth parents?" Hunter pressed, ignoring her question.

Kylie frowned. "I would think that was pretty obvious by now."

His lips quirked up. "So far all your reactions have been way different than I had expected, so sorry sweetheart, but there is nothing 'obvious' about you at all."

I'm not your 'sweetheart,' Kylie bristled, but she managed to keep her irritation from her expression. Now was not the time to unnecessarily butt heads with him. She needed to concentrate on getting as much information as she could about him, how much power he truly wielded within his clan, as well as stalling for time.

"Keep smirking like that and I won't answer any

more of your questions at all," she warned. "In fact, what even gives you the authority to barge into my home demanding answers in the first place? Those elders you mentioned earlier? Are you some kind of underground shifter cop who answers to only them?"

He made a face. "God no, but the Riverford PD *does* have a few shifters on the force. Which brings me back to the reason why you're currently in deep shit. As I mentioned before, the man you shredded lived. He's currently in the ICU of St. Agnes's Hospital babbling about God sending a girl who turned into a 'leopard' in order to punish him for what he had done to a shit-ton of other girls."

"So he *does* have something to do with all those missing women that have been all over the news lately," Kylie interjected softly, not able to stop the cold shudder that rippled through her body.

"Probably," Hunter agreed. "The bastard was practically begging to confess *something* at the very least, and because the pair of detectives sent down to the hospital happened to include a shifter, the elders of *all* the Riverford shifter clans know that there was a breech of secrecy. The only reason why they aren't here and I am is because everything you did last night happened within *my* territory, and like it or not, it makes you my responsibility above all others.

"You're lucky—not only that your body picked

that moment to shift for the first time, but that the bastard's system was pumped so full of a cocktail of illegal shit that it's a wonder he could even stand up straight. Everyone that heard him ranting on and on about his victim turning into an animal just assumed it was the ravings of a druggie tripping out after getting attacked by a mountain lion or bear. As I said before, we can fix this—if you'll let me. But you'll have to plead your case before the Elders. There's no getting around that."

"And if I don't?" Kylie said slowly. "If I refuse to see them, to have *anything* to do with your clan or shifters in general?"

Hunter flashed her a sad smile. "I hope for your sake, sweetheart, that you don't force me to show you the answer."

CHAPTER SIX

*K*ylie was over the arm of the couch and halfway to her bedroom before she heard Hunter's surprised curse, immediately followed by the thump of his shoes hitting the floor heavily as he had likely leapt over the back of the couch as well. Screw stalling. She had heard enough. His implied threat was all the answer she needed. There was no way she could trust any of the shifters. She had to get out of there!

Earlier, she had purposely opened her window while she had been alone in her bedroom in case she had to make a run for it. Her window faced the courtyard of the apartment complex, but more importantly, the small building that housed the manager's office was only about fifty yards away. If she could just make it out the window, at the very least, Hunter would not dare shift in such an open place where anyone looking out their window could see him. With a pursuer only on two feet, Kylie had a better chance of making it to that office, and maybe the humans inside, by their presence alone, would protect her.

Why, *why* had she not escaped earlier while she'd had the chance? No amount of information Hunter *might* have provided her should have been worth the risk of having no escape at all!

With speed driven by panic, Kylie made it through her bedroom door, intent on diving through the window, when what felt like a battering ram hit her squarely from behind, sending her crashing to the carpet with a cry of dismay. She opened her mouth to scream for help, but a large hand clamped over her mouth before she could utter a sound.

Still unwilling to give up, Kylie tried to bite him, but Hunter just pressed his hand harder against her mouth and adjusted his body until his full weight stretched out flat across her back pinned her completely to the floor. She tried to buck him off, to thrash her arms and legs, but she wasn't able to move her body more than a millimeter or two off the floor no matter how hard she strained up against him.

"I'm sorry, but I really can't let you leave,"

Hunter said into her ear, his tone genuinely apologetic, damn him. "I know you're scared and confused, but please just calm down. Let me help you, Kylie."

Kylie went limp beneath him, angry and feeling utterly defeated. After a tense, silent pause where neither one of them moved, Hunter cautiously removed his hand from her mouth, but he made no move to get off her. He was right not to trust her, she admitted grudgingly to herself, but that acknowledgment did nothing to lessen the bitterness welling up within her.

Things had been going so well these past twelve years after the agony and sadness of *that* night. College was great, and she had a circle of friends that she really cared about, as well as Paul. She had finally started to feel a sense of safety after none of the things she had feared all her life had occurred. Now, because of one sick bastard, that sense of safety had been thoroughly shattered, and Kylie despaired of ever regaining it.

"I don't want anything to do with all this craziness," Kylie finally said into the heavy silence.

Hunter sighed, his breath warm against the back of her neck, making her involuntarily twitch.

"You can't go back to living as just a human," he said gently. "Even now, the scent of your jaguar is getting much stronger. Other shifters will smell it and know you are one of us. It's dangerous for you to be left as you are now, ignorant of everything a shifter life entails, for both you and the shifters of this city. I could see it in your eyes last night, in your scent, when you faced off against me while we were both in jaguar form. The cat was almost completely in control, and that is something you can never let happen again."

"You make it sound as if I'm possessed by some sort of cat spirit, a demon…"

"Don't worry. It's nothing as sinister as that," Hunter assured her. "You see, we shifters have dual souls. Our human souls are naturally stronger, so I guess you can say human is our default state. Only a bit of the animal is allowed to seep through into our consciousness, to rule our instincts, but last night when I looked into your eyes for the first time, I couldn't see anything that was human. It's a wonder that your human soul was able to come back to the forefront at all."

Kylie closed her eyes, remembering her close call with the teenager in the street. She suddenly felt as exhausted as she had last night.

"Are you saying that I won't be able to keep the jaguar from coming out and taking over my mind?"

"I'm saying that without our help, my clan I

mean, that very possibility will hover over you every day for the rest of your life."

Hunter rose from her back and climbed to his feet. Kylie slowly pulled herself up onto her knees and looked up at the hand he held out to her.

Instead of accepting it, she raised her eyes to his face. "Can you promise me—can you promise me that if I go with you to see your elders, your clan won't lock me up somewhere like some kind of prisoner?"

"We haven't had a Returner in our clan for over a hundred years," Hunter said with a smile. "The last thing those old pussies would want is to alienate a new potential clan member." His expression turned wry. "Especially a female one."

Kylie stiffened. "If they think they can make me marry one of you—"

Hunter's sharp laugh cut her off. "The Elders may wish they could dictate all hookups within our clan, but trust me, if they ever tried, every single one of us would just give them the finger. No, what I meant was that the ratio of jaguar males to females in this city is three to one, so any addition of a lovely lady is always welcome."

Her shoulders relaxed slightly, and she slowly reached up to accept his hand up. Still backed into a corner, Kylie really wanted to trust him, but it would take more than a charming smile and a gorgeous face to break through years of always second guessing everyone's motives. She glanced over at the open window, and she abruptly felt Hunter squeeze her hand tightly. A warning.

With a weary sigh, Kylie turned her attention back to Hunter and deliberately pulled her hand from his grip. She was a little surprised that he let her without any real resistance.

"What now?" she asked.

He regarded her thoughtfully. "I need to explain a few more things and then I'll take you to speak with the Elders," he said.

A sudden, loud knock at the door had Kylie nearly jumping out of her skin and Hunter turning towards the door with what was unmistakably a low growl.

"Are you expecting anyone?" Hunter demanded, his entire body visibly tense.

A relief like no other instantly washed through her being, nearly making her knees give out. "Yeah, my—"

"Morning sweetie! It's me," Paul's soothing baritone called through her front door.

Kylie automatically started to move towards the door. He had used the code word, the one signifying that it was safe to open the door. However, before she could take more than a couple of steps, Hunter grabbed her arm.

"Don't answer that," he whispered warningly. "If it's your boyfriend, you can just call him later after all of our business is settled."

Kylie shook her head even as she strained against the hand wrapped around her arm. "I don't have a boyfriend. That's my dad, Paul."

CHAPTER SEVEN

$\mathcal{K}$ylie saw Hunter's nostrils flare as he stared hard at the front door.

"As I thought," he murmured. "He's human."

"He's here to pick me up for lunch," she lied. "My car is in the parking lot. He'll think something's up if I don't answer the door."

Hunter flashed her a skeptical look even as his hand tightened around her arm. "He'll just think you left with a friend."

Kylie shook her head. "I would never bail on my dad without calling him first. The only time I didn't was when I was in a car accident. He's somewhat of a worrywart, so he'll just think the worst." She clutched at Hunter's arm and did her best to make her eyes pleading. "Let me answer the door, *please!* If I suddenly become unreachable, he'll freak out and come looking for me. He might see something he's not supposed to, and I don't want him to get hurt because of me!"

When he still looked unconvinced, Kylie added, "The best thing right now is for me to go to lunch with him and pretend that I wasn't nearly tortured and murdered by some sick bastard last night, much less that I turned into a freaking jaguar! You can follow us, and afterwards, I'll go with you wherever you want as long as you promise me that you'll leave my dad out of all of this."

"Kylie!" Paul called again, his voice tinged with anxiety. He pounded on the door three more times in rapid succession.

She grabbed his free hand urgently. *"Please…"*

Hunter looked over at the door once more, before he slowly nodded without a word and released her arm.

Kylie closed her eyes briefly in relief. "Thank you," she whispered sincerely.

More pounding sounded, and she hurried over to the door before Paul decided to break it down. She sensed more than heard Hunter retreat into her bedroom.

"Coming Dad!" she called cheerfully, and the pounding abruptly ceased.

She never called Paul "dad."

"What did I tell you?" Paul scolded as soon as she opened the door.

"I know, I know," Kylie said apologetically as she stepped aside to let him in, "but this time I swear I was ready. I must've just dozed off for a minute at my desk waiting for you."

Paul's pale blue eyes surreptitiously swept the whole room as he entered the apartment. Taking advantage of her back being turned to Hunter's potential spying, Kylie gestured towards the bedroom with her eyes.

His eyes narrowed. "You've got to stop pushing yourself so hard, sweetie. Studying is important, but making time for sleep is even more so."

Kylie looped her arm through his and laughed. "But I always make time for lunch. Let's go. I'm starved."

As they headed for the door, Paul abruptly paused and said, "Don't forget your keys."

Her eyes followed his hand as he pointed down to the floor at her keys and cell phone, both still exactly where she had dropped them after collapsing earlier.

"Oh! They must've fallen out of my backpack when I came in last night."

Truthfully, she had forgotten all about them.

The last thing she needed was for Hunter to go through all her contacts and old texts.

After leaving the apartment, neither one of them said another word until they were inside his car and out of the parking lot.

"A shifter was there," Kylie said to his unspoken question, "a guy named Hunter Rivera from the local jaguar clan. He's following us right now. That's the only reason why he let us leave. I convinced him that we had a lunch date and that it would be better to go about my day normally."

"He's the one who saw you?" Paul guessed.

"Yeah. After I called you, I barely made it into my apartment before passing out. He literally sniffed me out and barged into my apartment just as I had finally become conscious again."

"I'm so sorry, Kylie," Paul said, sounding stricken. His hands gripped the steering wheel so tightly that his knuckles had turned white. "There was fog this morning, and my plane was delayed for almost three hours."

Kylie reached over and squeezed his upper arm. "You're here now. That's all that matters to me," she said, her voice rough with emotion.

Paul swallowed thickly and flashed her a tiny smile. "I'll drive us towards downtown. The lunch hour traffic should give you enough time to tell me everything. We'll decide what to do from there."

For the next twenty minutes, Kylie recounted the whole terrible episode, the terrifying realization that her abductor likely planned on using the scissors to cut more than her clothes, even confessing about how close she had come to attacking the teenagers she had stumbled upon afterwards. By the time she finished, Kylie was shaking so badly that she wrapped her arms around herself in an effort to control the tremors. Listening to Paul's words of comfort also helped soothe her wounded soul.

"Mom and Dad never once told me that holding on to their humanity while in their shifted forms was so hard," Kylie remarked softly.

"For them, I don't think it was," Paul replied carefully. "Although he rarely did so, whenever Alan would shift in front of me, I never felt as though I was in the presence of an animal. I think it was because no matter what he did, I could always see the human in his actions."

She hugged herself more tightly. "I'm scared, Paul. Hunter says that he only wants to help me, but he also says that he came after me because I broke some major shifter law by shifting in front of that psycho."

Paul glanced at her sharply. "What exactly has he told you?"

"He says that I have to go with him to talk to the elders of his clan, but it sounds more like I'm a criminal about to be put on trial!"

Paul sighed. "I hesitate to say you were lucky after everything you went through last night, but you were extremely lucky that piece of scum took you into a jaguar's territory. From what your father told me, the jaguar shifters of this city are good people, if a little bit solitary."

"What are you saying? That I should actually *let* Hunter take me to his clan's elders?" Kylie asked incredulously. "What if they ask me to shift, and I can't do it? Or worse, what if I screw up and they find out the truth about me? I have *no idea* how I shifted in the first place! It just—happened. Wouldn't it be better for me to run? I know you don't know where either my dad's or mom's clans are living, but now that I've shifted, shouldn't I try to find them?"

"Kylie—" Paul said, the hesitancy in his voice making her stomach clench in dread. "I didn't tell you this because I didn't want to needlessly worry you, but I've recently discovered that several Sniffers have managed to infiltrate the city."

Kylie sucked in a sharp breath. "How many?" she demanded.

"I don't know," Paul replied grimly. "Karen said that word on the street was that there were at least four confirmed and a dozen more suspected. There's no way that a shifter leaving the city with a human would go unnoticed, and I'd sooner cut off my left leg than let you try to leave alone. At this point, the best course would be to integrate with the jaguars, to let them act as your shield while we both try to gather more information. Up to this point, we've only had access to information coming from Riverford's cougar shifter clan. Adding the jaguar clan as allies would be a major boon. Lord knows we haven't gotten any closer to finding out what happened to your parents over the past few years."

"If the lions have actually managed to sneak their people into Riverford under such a careful watch, then don't you think the jaguars will be doubly suspicious of a 'human' like me suddenly shifting for the first time in adulthood?" Kylie asked. "Hunter insinuated that this is something that doesn't happen very often. They'll start to dig deeper into my past. Even without the suspicion, you know how important bloodlines are to shifters. I'm not so sure we should risk that level of scrutiny."

"Better the jaguars than the lions," Paul said firmly. "You did say that Hunter fellow told you all the various shifter clan elders in the alliance were informed about you and that Hunter was instructed to bring you in. I can't imagine something as serious as a breech of secrecy would be discussed beyond that level of hierarchy. If you present yourself before the jaguar clan elders willingly, then we can use that to our advantage. They must believe that you're a—forgive me—Deadend. Given the various social stigmas associated with that word, I don't think they'll see anything wrong with you asking them to keep that part of your history a secret. Let them spread a partial truth—that you are a shifter that revealed yourself to a human in order to save your life."

Paul reached over and grasped her hand, giving it tight squeeze. "This could be a good thing, sweetie."

Kylie flashed him a tiny smile. "I imagine Hunter expected lunch to end with a lengthy car chase. He'll be thrilled."

"It's too bad, though," Paul said with a sigh of—regret? "I've always wondered if participating in a car chase was as much fun as the movies made it look."

Kylie couldn't tell if her adoptive father was joking or not.

CHAPTER EIGHT

*A*fter eating lunch at a little Italian restaurant downtown, Paul drove Kylie back to her apartment.

"I'll do my best to keep my cell on me at all times," she said as she unbuckled her seatbelt. "If my phone starts tracking somewhere weird on the locator app or you don't hear from me by midnight, then just assume the worst has happened and call the cops."

"No one at work knows that I'm back in town yet," Paul said, "only that I left the conference because of a family emergency. I can stay at home for the next few days just watching that locater app if I need to." He smiled wryly. "Heck, if I have to go out, it's not as though anyone will look askance at me for staring at my phone screen overly long."

Kylie chuckled and reached for the door handle. She paused.

"Are you sure we're doing the right thing?" she asked, looking back at him a little anxiously.

"Sure? Absolutely not," Paul said seriously, "but given how you suddenly shifting after all this time has thrown pretty much everyone who knows for a loop, I do think this is the best course for now. I'll talk to Karen again this evening and see if anything new has come up regarding the Sniffers along the cougar grapevine."

He reached over and squeezed her shoulder affectionately. "Just keep your chin up and your eyes sharp as always. This may indeed turn out to be a good thing for you."

"I hope so," Kylie replied grimly.

"Once things settle down, we'll talk more about the other."

"Other?"

Paul's eyes flashed momentarily with anger. "The bastard that gave you that knot on your head."

Kylie flinched. After initially telling him about her attack and abduction in the vaguest of terms, she had been trying her damndest not to think about it at all. Although shifters healed three times as fast as regular humans, the large bump on her forehead was still very much visible. She only hoped it would disappear before she went back to class.

Her mouth twisted. If the jaguars even allowed her go back to class.

"Okay," she agreed, not quite able to hide the reluctance in her voice.

She hurried out of the car before her composure crumbled, waving her goodbye as Paul pulled away. Then nervously, she glanced around the lot. Although she had been watching all the cars tailing them down the freeways and streets through the side mirror, Kylie hadn't figured out which vehicle was Hunter's. She had also not seen any vehicles pull into the parking lot after them.

He probably just parked down the street, Kylie reasoned as she turned to head towards her apartment.

For all she knew, Hunter could already be waiting for her inside. She frowned as it occurred to her that he might have left her apartment unlocked when he had left to follow Paul and her.

Just as she reached her unit and was about to reach for the doorknob, Kylie suddenly felt a shiver go down her spine. She whirled around, her heart in her throat and her hands already instinctually rising up in defense before she let them fall back to her sides with a scowl.

"Good. It would have been embarrassing if you hadn't sensed you were being stalked," Hunter said with a smirk, standing only about a foot away from her.

"Not half as embarrassing as you're about to look writhing around on the asphalt and clutching your balls if you don't wipe that smirk off your face *right now*," Kylie growled. "What if you had made me accidentally turn into a jaguar again?"

"That's exactly what I was testing," he said.

She stared back at him incredulously. "Why would you do that while I'm outside? You were the one who made such a stink about being seen in the first place!"

"Which is why I waited until you were beneath the porch roof to approach you," he replied. "Unless someone is directly behind us, anyone standing underneath is hidden from view."

Kylie turned back to the door. "Please don't ever do that again," she said quietly as she dug her keys out of her pocket. "I'm probably going to have nightmares about that psycho attacking me from behind for the rest of my life, and I don't need any more reminders."

Hunter's hand was suddenly on her wrist, pleasantly warm against the iciness of her skin, making her pause before she could insert her key into the lock. "I think it would be best if we go see the Elders right now. They'll have more news regarding the asshole that kidnapped you. Maybe it'll give you some closure."

She turned back to him. "Where exactly will you be taking me?" she asked, letting suspicion creep into her voice.

"To the forest on the other side of the river along the outskirts of the city," he replied.

"So—what—one of the Elders has a house out there, or do you jaguars have some sort of secret lair?"

"A house, no. The Elders stay in a pretty sweet cave deep within the forest," Hunter said seriously.

Kylie stared at him. He *had* to be pulling her leg.

"You must be joking."

"'Fraid not." He looked her up and down. "In fact, it can get pretty chilly, so you might want to go grab a coat."

So he was the teasing type. Maybe. On any other day, she probably would have humored him, but right now she was in no mood for his or anyone else's games. She would call his bluff—if bluff it was.

"Forget it," she said stonily as she jammed the key into the lock. "You must be high if you think I'm going to follow a guy I barely know into a cave deep in the forest to meet a bunch of people I have no way of knowing even exist."

She managed to open the door before Hunter grabbed her arm. She had expected him to panic, to plead, or even apologize. That's why she was thrown a bit off-balance when he doubled over laughing.

"I'm sorry, but the look on your face…" he managed to get out between wheezes as Kylie glared daggers at him. "I take it you're not the outdoorsy type?"

"I like the outdoors just fine," Kylie retorted, jerking her arm out of his grip. "I just don't want to end up as the latest missing persons report on the six o'clock news tonight."

"You're right," Hunter said, swallowing his remaining laughter. "That was incredibly insensitive of me wasn't it? My brother—well never mind. I'm sorry that I upset you. I'm not really taking you to a cave, I promise."

Kylie folded her arms across her chest. "Then where?"

"One of the Elders is Donald Gaither."

Kylie started. His was a well-known name in Riverford society, the CEO of a major architectural firm. This was something Karen had never told them!

Hunter's lips quirked up. "We'll be going to his office downtown. The rest of the Elders should already be there waiting for us."

She hadn't exactly expected something like the Batcave, but she also had not expected to be taken to a regular office building either. The thought of going somewhere so public eased some of her tension. It was still the middle of the day, so the building would no doubt be filled with workers—potential witnesses. They couldn't *all* be shifters, could they?

"Come on. My truck is parked across the street. We can talk more on the way over."

"Fine." Kylie shut and relocked the door. "Why didn't you just park in the parking lot? I knew you were following us, so why all the subterfuge?"

Hunter raised an eyebrow. "You don't smell it?"

Kylie laughed humorlessly. "What *don't* I smell now? You'll have to be more specific."

"It's something sweaty and—oh, I suppose you can say aggressive. There really is no comparison to something a human can smell, so it's hard to explain."

As they began walking to the front of the apartment complex, Kylie inhaled deeply. She instantly wrinkled her nose as the plethora of both familiar and unfamiliar scents strengthened to the point of being nauseating.

"I can smell lots of things that could be described as sweaty," she replied.

He shrugged. "Then I suppose that's one of the first things you'll need to learn—how to recognize the different types of shifters by smell alone. While the scent of a jaguar can be rather pleasant, I can't say the same for all the others with the exception of maybe the other feline-types."

Kylie tensed. "Are you saying that you smell other shifters around here?"

"I really hope that you're near the end of your lease," Hunter said, "because there's no way you can get away with living in this apartment complex for longer than another day or two."

Now Kylie was really alarmed. Exactly what types of shifters had she been sharing a roof with?

"I have no idea what types of animals people might be able to shift into," she lied. "Are there dangerous ones living around here?"

Hunter nodded approvingly. "For a jaguar, yes. This area is the territory of Riverford's black bear clan, and let's just say that bears and jaguars don't exactly get along. They aren't nearly as bad as the alligator clan, but that's a tale better told later."

"Alligators…" Kylie said faintly, feigning shock since she figured it was a reaction Hunter might expect.

Hunter's lip curled up in disgust. "A shifter clan with almost no redeeming qualities save one."

When he didn't elaborate, Kylie prodded, "Which is…?"

His expression was suddenly guarded. "I'll tell you some other time."

Kylie fought to hide her frustration. It seemed she would have to work harder to get him to part with any information that would truly be useful to Paul and her, especially when he answered with the equivalent of the "I'll tell you when you're older" bullshit that parents often fed to their young children when asked uncomfortable questions. Still, it at least told her there was something worth digging into in regards to the local alligator clan.

Once they were in his black F-150 truck and well on their way down the freeway, Kylie ventured a question, "So, just so I have this straight, are jaguars expected to, I don't know, 'check in' with your elders every once in a while?"

"Do they keep us on leashes, you mean?" Hunter replied dryly.

Kylie merely raised an eyebrow and looked back at him expectantly.

"I think you have the wrong idea about what it means to be part of a shifter clan. What you're describing is more along the lines of being a member of a cult when the clans are nothing more than an extended family of sorts, a community. We don't bow down to the Elders as if they're kings or crap like that. They're just overseers to the interests of the clan as a whole."

"If that's true, then why do I feel like I've just been picked up by a cop and I'm on my way to the station to be interrogated?" she said pointedly.

He grinned sheepishly. "I suppose you're right, but yours is a special case. Bringing a Returner into the fold is a delicate affair all on its own, but add to that a breach of secrecy—well, sorry but we just can't risk leaving you up to your own devices. Imagine for a moment that the humans ever found out about us, the chaos it would likely cause."

Kylie made a face. "I would imagine that we'd find ourselves either hunted or strapped to a dissecting table in some underground government facility. Well, you don't have to worry about me blabbing about any of this to anyone, not even to my father. I'd likely end up in a psyche ward—wait— what do you mean 'returner'? You've used that word once before."

"You remember what I said about Deadends, that they were often sent to live with humans? Well, normally their kids are all born as humans. However, once in a blue moon, a human child with at least one shifter ancestor, no matter how far back in their lineage, can be born as a shifter. Those are known as

Returners and are very prized within the clans as they bring new genes into the community. Shifters only make up around one percent of the world population, so you can see that any new addition would be cause to throw a party."

"So—I'm not a Deadend?"

He shook his head. "There's really no way of knowing for sure until we find out who your parents were. I've never heard of a Deadend suddenly developing the ability to shift later in life, but I suppose there's a first time for everything. You being a Returner makes more sense. Either way, it would be better for you to be introduced to the rest of the clan as a Returner."

"And after today, will I be able to go back to my life? I'm missing all my lectures today, you know," Kylie said. "Midterms are coming up at the end of next week. I really can't afford to miss another day. I'm just lucky today wasn't a lab day. Those are a real pain in the ass to make up."

"Senior?" Hunter asked, sounding genuinely curious.

"Junior," she corrected.

Kylie hesitated. Maybe if she offered more information about herself first, then he would be more inclined to share more. She still needed to find out how Hunter figured into the jaguar clan's hierarchy.

"I'm a biology/pre-med major," she added.

"Hmm…so that makes you what? Twenty, twenty-one?"

"Twenty. What about you? What does a jaguar shifter do besides barge into apartments uninvited? Are you in college?"

Hunter laughed. "Not the best first impression, I'll give you that. No, I'm not a student. I manage a few apartment buildings and rental homes in my territory if you can believe it."

Kylie blinked in surprise. "That's the last thing I would've guessed."

He shrugged. "My family's always been in real estate."

"So—if I hadn't shifted while in your 'territory,' then would someone else have come after me?"

"You still think I'm some sort of underground cop don't you?" Hunter said in amusement.

Her eyes narrowed. "Laugh all you want, but how would you feel if you woke up today and found out your reality had become the real nightmare?"

His smile instantly disappeared as he turned to glance at her briefly with a completely unreadable expression in his eyes.

"Is the thought of turning into an animal really so horrible to you?" he asked.

"No," she answered without hesitation, "but the thought of accidentally ripping someone's throat out because I might not be able to control that part of me is."

"I don't think that's going to be a problem, to be honest," he said, his voice returning to its earlier friendlier tone. "You didn't lose control even a little bit when I startled you outside your apartment. We'll test it some more, of course, once we meet with the Elders."

"Why do I need to shift at all?" Kylie asked, genuinely curious about how he would answer. "Do shifters get sick or something if they don't change at least every once in a while?"

"Time'll answer that question better than I ever could. As I said before, don't think of shifting as being possessed by an animal. Part of you is human, yes, but the jaguar is equally who you are. Your nature is both. Once the shock of all this wears off, you'll likely find yourself longing to run through the forest, to hunt, as a jaguar."

Hunter paused for a long moment, then glanced over at her, his expression thoughtful.

"After your business with the Elders is finished, I can take you on a trial run through my personal patch of forest if you want," he offered a bit hesitantly.

"Don't you have better things to do than to babysit me?" Kylie asked slowly.

"I think hearing about a couple of stopped up toilets and the latest sob story about why so-and-so'll be late with next month's rent can wait until tomorrow," he said with a grin. "Unless it's something you'd rather do alone…"

Kylie really wished he wouldn't smile at her like that. It made her want to trust him too much, and that was something she could ill afford right now. However, she also couldn't afford to offend what could turn out to be a good ally.

She offered him a tiny smile. "I'll think about it."

CHAPTER NINE

The moment Kylie stepped inside the architectural firm, a wave of scents came crashing down on her, making her head swim so much that she had to grab onto Hunter's arm for a moment in order to steady herself.

"Hey, what's wrong?" Hunter asked, his brows knitting in concern as he pulled her off to the side.

"Ugh…how can you stand it?" she muttered, closing her eyes for a moment. "It's like walking into a perfume store after a tornado in here. Is it because there are a lot of shifters here? The smells weren't nearly as in-your-face earlier when I was in the restaurant with my dad!"

"Your body must still be adjusting," he soothed. "Everything should balance out within a few days.

Until then, when you're around a lot of people, try breathing shallowly."

Kylie nodded. It was a testament to how overwhelmed she was feeling that she didn't even try to pull her hand away when he took it. It was even a bit steadying.

They took the elevator up to the top floor. The doors opened up to a large reception room that was surprisingly empty except for the lone receptionist at her desk in the center of the room. Her expression was openly surprised.

"Mr. Rivera, we weren't expecting you and your guest for at least another couple of hours," she said, glancing at Kylie curiously.

Kylie mentally snorted. *"Guest" my ass!*

"We can leave and come back if the Elders aren't ready for us," Hunter offered.

"No, no," the receptionist said quickly. "If you both will just have a seat, I'll inform them that you're here. It shouldn't be long."

"I should've asked earlier, but how many elders are there in the jaguar clan? Or is it the same amount in all the clans?" Kylie questioned as they sat down.

"Every clan is different," Hunter replied, "and while only the members of each clan truly know how many elders govern them—and sometimes even *they* aren't completely sure of the whos and how manys—

the jaguars currently have ten. I hesitate to call him the head honcho, but Donald Gaither is the Elders'—voice, I suppose is a good way of putting it. Step out of line or if there's anything important to report, then it'll be him you'll likely be talking to."

"He's rumored to be cold and unfriendly."

Hunter smirked. "Tell him that and you'll make his day. If he were a wolf shifter, then saying his bark was worse than his bite would've been the perfect description of his personality. He's just really aloof, and that's saying something when talking about jaguar shifters. Socialization isn't very high on our list of pastimes. With the exception of our mates and children, it's just our nature to walk alone."

"I love to hang out with my friends. Now that my jaguar half has been—activated, will being around a lot of people start to irritate me?" Kylie asked worriedly.

"I don't know about irritate, but you might start to feel uncomfortable. Surround a cat with potential enemies, and the first thing he'll want to do is find an escape route. Or a door in a shifter's case. That being said, it's just an instinctual feeling and is not so strong that you can't easily ignore it. Like all the new things you've smelled today, it just takes some getting used to."

The receptionist returned, and Hunter instantly

rose to his feet, leaving Kylie to scramble after him. "They're in the largest boardroom."

"Good. That means we can sit," Hunter said, smiling at Kylie. "Follow me."

He led her through a set of double doors to the left of the reception desk into a narrow hall lined with what were probably individual offices. They walked to the end, and Hunter knocked soundly on the door once before he opened it without waiting for a response.

Kylie swallowed against the knot of anxiety that had suddenly formed in her throat and reluctantly followed Hunter into the room. Her eyes immediately did a sweep of the room, noting that there were six women and five men seated all along a long table of cherry oak, before her eyes fell on the somewhat familiar graying man that was seated at the far end. She had seen him a few times at some of the fundraisers she had accompanied Paul to over the years.

"You've caused quite the stir, young lady," Donald Gaither said in lieu of a greeting, his dark eyes boring into her as Hunter and she stood behind the empty chair at the other end of the table.

"Not by choice," Kylie replied stiffly, not daring to break eye contact with him.

He nodded. "Given the circumstances, you

should be applauded. The police have had some time to look into your attacker. That human was quite the piece of work. However, we'll get to all of that soon enough. I think introductions are in order first."

One by one, all the Elders introduced themselves by name and occupation. One, Kylie was startled to realize once she got a good look at him, was a history professor she'd had at the university as a freshman. The husband and wife duo sitting next to him were elementary school teachers. Another woman was a police detective. The rest represented a variety of careers from mail carrier to business owners like Mr. Gaither.

Rather than some kind of elite club that Kylie had totally expected, the Elders were a surprising group of individuals that truly represented the different types of people within a community well. Kylie felt some of the tension ease from her shoulders.

"You were one of my students, were you not?" Professor Martinez asked after Kylie had introduced herself.

She nodded. "Intro to World History, yes."

"Interesting. You never once gave off the scent of a jaguar or else I would have noticed. We sometimes get a few jaguar shifter students from Mexico, South and Central America, or Arizona, but not so many that you, as an unfamiliar face, would have been overlooked. I enjoy chatting about the differences and similarities in our clans."

Kylie shifted her feet uncomfortably. He was showing much more interest in her than she would have liked. A history professor could prove to be especially dangerous, more so if he saw her as a puzzle to be solved.

"Indeed. That such a trauma could awaken your dormant jaguar soul from such a near absolute human state," Mr. Gaither said, looking every bit as interested as the professor.

Kylie swallowed thickly. Or was that suspicion? Suddenly it felt way too hot and confining in the room. She briefly wondered if they would chalk it up to being so new to shifting if she followed all the instincts that were screaming for her to get the hell out of there and darted from the room just like Hunter had mentioned earlier.

"Have you shifted again since?" Professor Martinez asked.

"No. Everything's so crazy right now that I haven't even considered it."

"*Can* you do it again?" Gaither asked shrewdly.

"I don't know," she answered, feeling that it was best to be honest here. "I have no idea how it happened in the first place."

"There's nothing to it," Hunter said, speaking for the first time since they had entered the boardroom. "Desire to be the cat is all you need. Just thinking about shifting with genuine intent behind it will usually do it."

"We wish to see you try," Mr. Gaither said. "Hunter, please take Miss Moore into the office next door so that she may remove her clothing and shift in privacy."

"Come on," Hunter said with a contrite smile, ushering her towards the door with a hand lightly pressing against her back.

"What will they do if I can't shift?" Kylie asked once they were back in the hall and Hunter had closed the door.

"I don't think that will happen, but on the off chance that it does, they'll probably just ask you to come back next week to give it another go. After all, none of us really knows what to expect with a Returner. Now, I'll be just outside the door. When you shift, give it a *whack* with your paw, and I'll know it's okay to open it."

With my paw... Kylie didn't think she would ever get used to hearing things like that.

After making sure the blinds were drawn across the huge window, Kylie began to undress, feeling utterly exposed. It was as though she was being initiated into one of those strange secret societies. She could only hope that all her discomfort would be worth it in the end.

Once naked, rather than dwell on all her fears of failure, Kylie took to heart all of Hunter's advice, got down on her hands and knees, and thought forcefully, *I want to shift!*

Immediately, her muscles began to quiver, and before she could gasp in surprise, Kylie felt her body stretch and contort familiarly in that huge muscle spasm she had experienced last time. It was over in a matter of a few seconds, and the first thing she noticed was that she could smell Hunter as keenly as though he was standing right next to her. Looking down, she was met with two black-spotted, gold and white paws.

A strange, chuffing sound came from her throat, the feline equivalent of a laugh, she supposed since she was as giddy as a teen on her first date. It was a completely strange experience to feel herself absently lashing her tail behind her. She was also surprised to find herself itching to go for a run, the walls of the office feeling a thousand times stuffier and more confining while in jaguar form.

Kylie instantly put the breaks on those kinds of thoughts. Her human mind was in control now, and she didn't want to risk losing control again by thinking like a jaguar. Besides, Hunter and a room full of elders were waiting for her, so any further explorations of her new form would have to wait for another time.

She trotted over to the door and gave it a sound *whack* with a paw. The door immediately opened to reveal a grinning Hunter.

"I told you, you didn't have anything to worry about," he said.

Kylie chuffed in agreement as she followed him back to the boardroom.

"Excellent," Mr. Gaither said as soon as they entered. "I'm happy that there aren't going to be any problems on that front. As long as you can shift back into your human form just as easily, then we can consider the matter resolved. Hunter, regarding that other problem you mentioned the last time we spoke, do you have any spare units in the building you reside in that you can offer her?"

"Yes."

"Good. We'll arrange movers to take care of the transition on Saturday. In the meantime, put her up in your guestroom. Under no circumstance should she return to that apartment for longer than it takes to grab a change of clothes." Gaither's eyes turned back to Kylie. "You can return back to the office to shift back now. When you return, we'll discuss the human who was the cause of all this as well as the laws within our clan."

Had she been in her human form, Kylie would have been hard-pressed not to make a face. Looks as though she wasn't as off the hook as she had thought.

***

"Sorry," Kylie said as Hunter and she left the office building a little over an hour later, "but right now I'd rather you just take me home. Having to tell them everything about that awful night and then having to listen to all of them drone on and on about shifter laws and etiquette the way they did was exhausting."

"Kylie…" Hunter looked down at her pointedly.

She sighed. "I know, I know. The big bad bears might eat me. Just drop me off by my car, and I'll go stay over at my dad's tonight. I'll tell him that there's a problem with the sewage line in my apartment. That way, he won't be so surprised when I move over to your building. I just need some time to myself to process all of this. Then tomorrow you can take me to meet everyone the Elders 'suggested.' My last class ends at five, and I should be home by five-thirty."

"…okay," he relented. "I'll pick you up around

seven. And after that, how about we take that run in the forest I suggested earlier?"

Kylie couldn't help smiling. He was so incorrigible.

"Maybe we can do that too."

CHAPTER TEN

"I'm not so sure I like the idea of you living so close to the river," Paul said as they headed out the door early the next morning. "The jaguars may claim the eastern half, but that's never stopped the alligators from pushing their boundaries."

"Don't worry," Kylie replied with a grimace. "Hunter's territory is in the easternmost portion, so there's no reason I'd go anywhere near the contested borders unless it was deliberate. Believe me, between all the horror stories my parents and Karen have told me about the alligator clan, you couldn't pay me to go even to the jaguar territories on the fringes of alligator territory."

"I'll talk to Karen at work and ask her to keep her ears open for anything gator related. They aren't part of the Alliance, but no doubt they've at least heard a few rumors about what happened the other night. I hate to say this, but I'm glad Hunter will be looking after you for the time being."

"Honestly, I'm surprised the Elders didn't make him into my bodyguard or something the way they went on and on about the significance of a Returner. The more Hunter tells me about the clan, the more I'm not so sure joining them was such a good idea. One of the Elders is a history professor at my university, and he looked positively gleeful at the prospect of searching for the identity of my parents."

Paul turned to unlock his car, but not before Kylie saw the troubled look in his eyes. "What's done is done. All we can do now is be extra cautious and try not to do anything that would draw the wrong kind of attention. Once all the excitement dies down a bit, then you can decide whether or not you want to stay here or if we should try to go to the British Isles to look for your mother's clan."

"Let's not think about that right now," she said. "I'll call you tonight after Hunter finishes introducing me to some of the local jaguars."

As Kylie drove to the university, she spent the whole way dreading the onslaught of scents she knew awaited her. She only hoped that Hunter would be right, that her newly enhanced sense of smell had leveled out somewhat overnight. Otherwise, she would have to miss another day of classes—which she could *not* afford—because there was no way she would be able to concentrate with her head spinning. She hadn't really noticed a difference with Paul's scent this morning, but…

As she waited at a red light, Kylie resisted the urge to start banging her head on the steering wheel. Sometimes life just *really* pissed her off, and she didn't need to add a headache to the whole horrible mix.

Besides, the ugly knot on her temple had all but disappeared when she had examined herself this morning. The last thing she needed to do was reintroduce *that* nasty little reminder of just how much life could screw you.

The moment Kylie stepped out of her car, the scents of thousands of people assaulted her senses just as she had feared. Determined not to give up, she stood by her car and just breathed slowly and shallowly as she had back at the architectural firm, letting herself get used to the maelstrom of acrid and earthy scents.

After a few minutes, her head stopped spinning and the smells not quite so potent.

Maybe I can do this after all.

Relieved, Kylie headed towards her first class,

hoping to catch her friend, Molly, before class started to borrow yesterday's notes.

***

"Are you sure you don't want to come?" Kylie's friend, Tara, persisted as Kylie walked with her, Molly, and Molly's boyfriend, Ty, towards the parking lot after their last class.

"It's not that I don't want to," Kylie said, pinching the bridge of her nose as if in pain. "It's just my head's been killing me since Genetics. I think yesterday's fever is back. I don't want to get any of you sick."

"Yeah, you are looking kinda pale," Molly said, peering back at her critically. "You probably should've stayed home today, too."

Kylie shook her head. "You know I hate making up labs. The prof probably would've made me come in on Sunday this time. By the way, thanks for the notes."

"No problem. Just make sure they stay in your backpack until at least tomorrow. You're probably long overdue for a good snooze."

"Yes, Mom," Kylie teased.

Molly snorted. "Yeah, laugh all you want, but that's probably why you got sick in the first place."

"We might go clubbing tomorrow night," Tara interjected. "Call me if you feel better, and I'll pick you up."

"Sounds like a plan."

Hopefully Hunter wouldn't have anywhere else she needed to go. Kylie had a feeling that her list of excuses to her friends would dry up pretty quickly otherwise.

If you have to go a lot of places with Hunter, then there's one excuse that would work for everything, her mind supplied helpfully.

The thought startled her. Then she was irritated with herself. There was no denying that Hunter was hot, but getting involved with him would probably be the worst thing she could do right now, especially when she hadn't even decided if she was going to stay or go hunting her mother's clan.

She snorted. As if getting involved with him was even a problem in the first place. He hadn't shown any romantic interest in her at all. Talk about counting your chickens before they hatch.

Once she was back at her apartment, Kylie began to pack up some of her things into the few boxes she had on hand while she waited for Hunter to arrive. The Elders had told her that they would take care of hiring movers to come on Saturday, and although she had nothing in the apartment that was dangerous for others to see, Kylie still didn't feel comfortable allowing total strangers to handle her more personal items.

While she worked, Kylie let her mind wander to all the potential jaguar shifters Hunter would soon introduce. At the very least, it would be interesting to see if any of them were people she actually knew. There were already a handful of people at her university that she was pretty sure were jaguar shifters. Jaguars and humans were the only two scents she was able to identify with any confidence. Hopefully Karen would be able to come over to Paul's for lunch on Sunday and she could add cougar to the list. The rest she would have to ask Hunter to help her with.

She was in the process of packing up the contents of her underwear drawer into a suitcase when she caught a whiff of a familiar scent. Her head was already up and scenting the air before she realized what she was doing. A bit unsettled, Kylie headed for the living room just as a loud knock sounded on the front door.

The scent of a jaguar was strong as she fumbled with the lock. She supposed it was a convenient way to know who—or what—was at the door before she bothered to answer it, but it still kind of freaked her out.

"Hi," Hunter said as soon as the door swung open, a smile lighting up his face, and to her horror, Kylie's heart instantly began to race in excitement.

What the hell was wrong with her? She had *never* reacted to a guy like that, no matter how hot he was.

Embarrassed, she smiled at him tightly before waving him inside. "Just let me go grab my purse and keys and we can go."

"You're just as tense and wary as the first time I stepped through this door," Hunter remarked. "Did something happen? A bear come sniffing already?"

Kylie pocketed her keys and cell phone and snatched her purse from the coffee table. "No, it's nothing like that. My jaguar side is just freaking me out right now."

Hunter raised an eyebrow. "How so?"

She shrugged uncomfortably. "I'm just not used to reacting to things the way a cat would. It makes me nervous because I'm not sure I *should* be acting that way at all, if maybe I'm letting too much of the jaguar come through."

Hunter's eyes softened in understanding. "You're still worried about losing control."

"Constantly," Kylie admitted, though with more meaning than Hunter could ever guess.

"You shifted forms back and forth with no problem with the Elders yesterday," Hunter reminded her.

Kylie smiled sheepishly. "I know. I keep telling myself that over and over, but—I guess it's because all of this shifter business still doesn't feel natural to me."

"With a few more shifts under your belt, it'll literally become your second nature," he assured her. "Now, we'd better head out. I'd like you to meet a good friend of mine who co-owns a local nightclub nearby, and I think, given your problems yesterday with your sense of smell, it would probably be better to see him now before it gets too crowded."

CHAPTER ELEVEN

"Your friend owns *Southern Glacier!*" Kylie exclaimed as Hunter drove around to the back of the large, illuminated building and entered the club's VIP parking garage.

She had expected Hunter to take her to one of the many small clubs along the edges of downtown that she and her friends often frequented, not *the* hottest club in Riverford.

"Co-owns," Hunter corrected with a grin.

"My friends and I have always wanted to come here," Kylie admitted, "but I always thought there was no way a bunch of lowly college students like us would stand a chance of getting in so we never tried."

"You'd be surprised," Hunter said. "The owners

aren't as fussy about their patrons as you might think. It's all just the luck of the draw as long as you're willing to wait in line long enough since people are selected randomly. Really, the owners would let everyone in if they had the room so long as you could pay the cover."

"Even alligator and bear shifters?" Kylie asked shrewdly.

Hunter smiled wryly. "You got me there. No, anyone from the alligator clan are most definitely not welcome. They're naturally—forgive the pun—*snappish*. They can't be trusted to not start trouble. Their tempers are always on a hair-trigger. That's one of the many reasons why they are always at odds with most of the other shifter clans."

"And the bears?"

"They can be aggressive when provoked just like their wild counterparts, but for the most part, as long as their boundaries are respected, they won't cause trouble just for the sake of causing trouble like the alligators. You might see a bear or two in the club, but they tend to not like crowds. Maybe a few jaguars will also show while we're here and I can introduce you."

"A lot of people at the university were staring at me today," Kylie said. "I'm not sure how many of them were jaguars, but I imagine they were shocked that someone that had been human a couple of days ago suddenly smelled like a jaguar."

"I don't think the Elders have gotten around to telling everyone in the clan about you. We don't gather very often, so that's what this little tour of introductions I'm taking you on is all about."

Kylie snorted. "Sounds to me like they're just dumping me on you. I mean, how hard can it be to rent a large hall and just call everyone up and say 'come meet the clan's new member'?"

Hunter chuckled. "Normally I would agree with you, but you're a special case. It's very unusual for a shifter to leave their clan for another unless it's for a mating, so new, unattached additions are pretty rare. It's tradition that they introduce themselves to key members of the clan, but since you're new to all of shifter society in general, it's only logical that they ask me, the only jaguar you're somewhat familiar with, to help you with the introductions."

"So one of the owners of this club is a key member of your clan?" she asked. Knowing just who filled the upper echelons of the jaguar clan could prove useful to her and Paul's search.

"Oh, no. Maxim—that's my friend—heard about you from a family member who's an Elder and wanted to meet you."

There was something about the way Hunter

grinned at her as he replied that immediately set Kylie on edge, but she couldn't for the life of her figure out why or even if it was *her* who noticed it or the jaguar in her. She was beginning to wonder if she would ever get used to her dual nature, that maybe she had lived as just a human for too long. What was the use of having enhanced instincts if she couldn't interpret any of their meanings?

Hunter stopped his truck in front of a group of young men dressed in black tuxedoes, and two of them immediately broke away to open their doors. The valet had the strong, earthy smell of a shifter, though it had another underlying element that she had never smelled before. Kylie wondered which type of shifter he was. She would have to remember to grill Hunter later about which shifters were friendly with whom and not just for appearances.

Loud music assaulted her senses once they stepped into the club, from a live band she was pleased to note. She wondered how long Hunter planned for them to stay. It was Friday night, after all, and she was missing out on hanging with her friends. Not that she had much to complain about seeing as she was currently walking into *Southern Glacier* with a super hot guy—and she did *not* just think that.

Kylie's entire body seemed to heat up as she

glanced at Hunter from the corner of her eye. Hadn't she already decided that she would keep their relationship strictly on friendly terms, that she wouldn't even try to flirt? It wasn't like her to fixate on any guy, no matter how hot, especially when she knew how dangerous letting this guy in particular get closer to her could be.

Even though it was fairly early as far as clubbing was concerned, the tables and dance floor were already pretty crowded. Never had Kylie been so glad about the city-wide ban on smoking in public places than now. She could only imagine the havoc adding cigarette smoke to her already reeling senses would have caused.

Hunter led her through the tables towards the huge bar that spanned the entirety of one of the far walls. He caught the eye of one of the many bartenders and spoke something into his ear that Kylie couldn't hear over the music.

"Have a seat," Hunter said, gesturing towards a barstool that someone had just vacated. "I sent that bartender after Maxim. If you want, I'll buy you a drink while we wait."

Kylie raised an eyebrow as she jumped up onto the stool. She beckoned Hunter closer and said into his ear, "I guess you forgot."

He tilted his head curiously. "Forgot?"

"I'm only twenty remember."

For a couple of seconds, he looked confused before he shot her an incredulous look. "Normally this would be the last place you'd want to bring that little fact to anyone's attention."

Her smile was self-deprecating. "I'm not much of a drinker." Let him make of that what he will, but the last thing she wanted to do was get into the "whys."

He nodded and then flashed her a smile that was much too charming for her peace of mind. "Even so, my offer still stands. Sparkling water? Coke? Italian soda?"

Kylie couldn't help returning his smile. "Thanks, but I'm good." She gestured with her chin over to the stage where the four-man band was just finishing up a rock song she had never heard before. "Being able to listen to live music is enough for me. I'm usually too busy with school, so it's not something I get to do as much as I'd like."

"Sounds exhausting," Hunter said, leaning up against the bar.

"It can be."

"I never had the 'pleasure' of going to college. When my parents died, my brother and I took over several apartment complexes and rental properties. Occasionally, I will even buy and flip a house. I guess you can say real estate is in my family's blood."

"Is your brother older or younger?"

"Older." Hunter's eyes flickered to the side briefly, his posture suddenly tense.

"You sound pretty busy yourself having to manage that much property," Kylie remarked, deciding not to press the subject. No use purposely stepping on a potential minefield—at least not yet. "I'm sorry that the Elders saddled you with me."

His lips curved up. "Because coming to Southern Glacier with a cute girl is so terrible."

"Well, that was certainly quick," a deep voice abruptly said loudly near Kylie's ear, startling her so much that she nearly fell off her stool.

"Don't even," Hunter said warningly at the tall, platinum blond man dressed completely in black in a fashionable suit sans tie who was smiling affably at them both.

A strong scent of something that was definitely not the scent of a jaguar shifter emanated from him, reminding Kylie of the clean smell of snow in the air. It completely caught her off-guard. She had automatically assumed Hunter's friend would be another jaguar, and now she realized how utterly short-sighted that was of her.

"Maxim Clarke," he offered, holding out a hand to her.

His large hand all but swallowed hers as they shook hands. "Kylie Moore. It's nice to meet you."

The moment she released his hand, Kylie felt a surge of warmth flow through her entire body. It took every ounce of control she had to keep from visibly reacting. What in the hell had just happened? Did Maxim do something to her? Exactly what type of shifter was he?

For his part, Maxim gave no indication that he knew she was freaking out inside, regarding her with the same polite interest in his pale blue eyes. Maybe it was just a natural reaction that shifters of certain clans experienced. Did she dare ask which clan he belonged to? Kylie turned and looked at Hunter questionably, hoping he would understand and save her from asking and possibly committing some kind of social *faux pas*.

"He's a tiger," Hunter said. There was a definite tinge of amusement in his voice.

"Siberian, to be exact," Maxim interjected. "We and the Bengal tiger clan have got a rivalry going on, so you don't want to get us confused."

"At this point, I wouldn't know a Bengal tiger shifter from a moose shifter—if there's even such a thing—so it'll probably be better for everyone all around if I just don't say anything," Kylie said wryly.

Maxim laughed. "Well, come to my family's club

often enough and you'll definitely get a nose-full. You'll find no better melting pot of shifters outside a university." He slapped Hunter on the back. "I'm sure this guy'll be happy to set you straight. I'm always telling him he needs to get out more, anyway."

"Your whole family runs the club?"

"Just my older brother, sister, and their mates. You'll find that with shifters, pretty much everything is either family or clan-oriented. Well, with the exception of the jaguar loners. They tend to do their own thing."

"And that's why we have more territory in this city than any other clan," Hunter said.

"Too true, but at least you're not greedy about it like those damn gators," Maxim said darkly.

Hunter's entire demeanor was instantly alert. "More trouble?"

The tiger shifter sighed. "Always," he replied, his tone heavy with meaning. He turned his attention back to Kylie. "The alligator clan hates us felines more than any other. As I'm sure your new clan's elders told you, a Returner like you is a big deal in the shifter world, like winning the genetic lottery. It's only a matter of time before the gators catch wind and see an opportunity to strike back where it would hurt most. When that happens, just know that the Siberians will have your back."

Kylie was taken aback. Was this the reason why Hunter wanted her to meet Maxim? Did she dare hope that she might have found more true allies within the shifters like Karen?

It was still too early to judge, but for the first time in a long time, Kylie felt a flutter of hope that maybe, just maybe she and Paul might be able to move their investigation into her parents' disappearance past the utter standstill it had been in for over a year now.

"Saying thanks doesn't seem like it's enough, but thanks," Kylie said.

He waved a hand dismissively. "I know all this must seem confusing as hell, so the least all of us can do is ease you into our world as painlessly as possible. Which reminds me—a gator tried to start a fight outside the club last Friday and lost his beanie in all the excitement. I'll have security bring it to you so you can get a whiff. That's one scent you'll want to know right away."

"I also have something I want your guys to look at," Hunter said.

"Of course. Did you want to do this now or..." Maxim's gaze flickered over to Kylie meaningfully before fixing on Hunter again.

"Kylie, do you want to go to the back with us, or—" Hunter touched her shoulder, and for the second time that night, Kylie nearly fell off her stool as that same strange warmth she had felt after shaking hands with Maxim shot throughout her body. However, this time it seemed much stronger, hotter and lingering, as though she had just submerged herself in a hot tub.

Hunter immediately sprang forward to steady her. "Kylie?" he asked worriedly.

"S-sorry," she said, shaking her head as if to clear it. "I just felt dizzy all of a sudden. It's probably just my senses going haywire again."

He frowned. "Maybe it was too soon to bring you into such a crowded place."

She smiled at him with forced reassurance. "I'm okay now. I was only dizzy for a second. You two go on ahead and take care of whatever business you have. I'll just sit here and listen to the band."

When Hunter hesitated, Maxim said, "Don't worry. I'll have a couple of my guys keep an eye on her."

"Okay, but you should at least drink something," Hunter insisted. "Just think of how it'd look if you passed out and I had to carry you out."

This time Kylie's smile was real. "You really do want to buy me that drink," she teased. "Fine. I'll have one of those cherry Italian sodas you mentioned earlier."

As Hunter waved over a bartender, Maxim turned to her and said, "You have a pretty strong scent. I can only imagine it's because you're a Returner. I've never met one before you so I can't compare, but it may peak a few shifters' curiosity."

He pointed to a couple of large men who looked like real bruisers standing at the other end of the bar. "I'll have those two make sure no one takes that curiosity any further."

"I appreciate it."

"I promise we won't be long," Hunter said with an apologetic smile as he and Maxim headed away from the bar.

Kylie watched the two men with narrowed eyes as they quickly wove through the throng towards the back of the room with the agility associated with the big cats who were, in essence, their alter egos. For some inexplicable reason, she suddenly had a strong desire to chase after them. Just thinking about going after them made her whole body heat up and buzz with—something. Excitement? She wasn't sure.

Now thoroughly freaked out, she tore her eyes away and concentrated on her drink and the live music. It was no doubt her jaguar side reacting to something beyond her human comprehension. Now was definitely not the time to lose control of her senses, surrounded by a sea of potential enemies.

She could only hope Hunter really wouldn't be gone long.

CHAPTER TWELVE

*I*t was only when she noticed a third pair of eyes, this time from one of the tables close to the bar, staring rather openly at her that Kylie's initial concern started to turn to fear.

The first was a guy sitting four stools down from her. One moment he was chatting with a couple of women, and the next, he froze before turning to look directly at her as if he had suddenly caught her scent in the air. Only—she was pretty sure that he and the rest of the people sitting around her were human.

The second was also a human, an older, thirtyish guy who happened to walk by her. He too had frozen mid-step as if someone had called out to him before turning to look at Kylie with something like bewilderment. This guy had slowly moved on, but sometime when her attention had been on the stage and the band, he had returned to the bar and was now seated at the very end not even trying to hide the fact that he was staring at her with a decidedly creepy expression.

Kylie watched all three warily, wondering if she should wave over the two security guys Maxim had pointed out. It had only been about twenty minutes since Hunter and Maxim had left her at the bar, so she was reluctant to cause a scene that may send them running back to her. There was also the chance that she might be seen as weak within the shifter society, and thus people would be more reluctant to share anything of value with her. Then the opportunity entering the jaguar clan presented would be wasted.

Her eyes flickered over to the security men, and she was a bit startled to see them already looking back at her with twin frowns stretching their lips. They were looking at her as though they didn't like something she was doing, but for the life of her, she couldn't fathom what. It wasn't as though she was encouraging all those creepy stares.

Just as Kylie shot them a puzzled look, a group of seven guys passed in front of them, blocking her view and capturing her full attention. In that moment, she was once again submerged in an inexplicable warmth, and as one, every single guy in that group turned to look at her.

Kylie flinched back in reaction, her heart suddenly speeding up in the beginnings of panic. Her eyes darted around them in an effort to alert the security guys that things had suddenly gone bat-shit crazy, and she inadvertently locked gazes with Creepy Guy Number One who was still sitting four stools down.

Before she could even blink, all seven guys converged on the stool guy, attacking him with fists and kicks. Kylie expected him to cry out for help, but instead, he let out a weird, guttural sound that was purely animalistic and returned blow for blow like a man possessed.

More men began to join the fray as Kylie jumped off the stool and turned with the intent of sprinting for the exit. Instead, she was met with a wall of at least eight men advancing on her with a look of hunger in their eyes like a starving vampire. To add to the horrors, as she crouched into a defensive position, a low growl began to rise on its own accord from deep within her throat, and she could already feel the slight spasms in her muscles that signaled her body was on the verge of shifting.

Shit! Shit!

"Kylie!"

The sound of Hunter's voice in that moment of chaos was as stunning as hearing a chorus of angels. Her head snapped towards his voice in enough time to see him lay out a tall blond guy with a brutal punch to the chin who had tried to block his advance.

She wasted no time in rushing to him, reaching out to grab his arms. "Hunter! What the *hell* is going on! I—"

The moment Kylie touched him, her entire body seemed to ignite with flames, and only Hunter's quick reflexes prevented her from crumbling to the ground. Desire, lust like she had never felt before inundated her mind, her senses, and she found herself lunging at Hunter with a very audible growl, intent on devouring that luscious mouth she had only admired from afar.

Yes—yes—he's the one!

"*Fuck!*" Hunter cursed, thrusting her out at arms-length and shaking his head violently as though to clear it after being punched.

"She doesn't know how to control it!" Maxim's voice penetrated the haze of lust that had almost completely taken over Kylie's mind as effectively as a gunshot in a library, causing her next growl to freeze in her throat. "Get her out of here *now*! I'll take care of things here!"

With another harsh curse, Hunter pulled her tightly against him and began to half-drag, half-march her through the surrounding crowd as fast as he could without sending them both to the ground. Enveloped within his warmth and now mouth-watering scent, Kylie's groin began to throb rather insistently with arousal. She groaned and tried to rub herself against him as they walked, but the constant movement of their legs prevented her from gaining any good friction.

The walk to the VIP entrance seemed to take an eternity, but thankfully Hunter's truck was already waiting for them outside at the curb, doors open and engine running, though the valets were conspicuously absent. By then, all Kylie could think about was getting inside, climbing onto Hunter's lap, and screwing him until they both passed out.

She tried to push Hunter through the opened passenger door, but he grabbed her head firmly between his hands and held steady until she was finally able to focus on his eyes.

"Kylie, you *have to calm the fuck down*," Hunter said sternly, his eyes hard and piercing. "You're in heat, sweetheart, and you're sending out enough mating pheromones to attract the whole state of Texas right now!" He paused and gritted his teeth. "It's taking everything I have in me to keep from ripping your clothes off and screwing you blind right here on the sidewalk," he continued roughly. "I have to get you out of here, but there's no way I'll be able to keep from driving us into a ditch when all I can think about is driving my cock into your body! Try to think of the most un-arousing things as possible…!"

Although she was able to hear every word and she suspected that he was purposely being blunt and crude to shock her, Kylie was having a hard time comprehending them when Hunter smelled *so damn good.* However, some of his desperation managed to seep into her awareness, and enough of Kylie's humanity still remained to want to understand that urgency to fight to the forefront of her consciousness. She was suddenly seeing Hunter as the human woman rather than the jaguar, could see the sweat on his brow and how his entire body shook with the effort of keeping himself from throwing her onto the ground and having his wicked way with her right then and there.

Kylie drew in a sharp, shocked breath, and some of the heat that was scorching her body from within began to cool. At that moment, Hunter looked more animal than man even though he was still in his human form.

I did this to him, Kylie realized with rising horror, *to those men.*

The pinched look on Hunter's face eased, and he slowly released her head and stepped back. His eyes were fixed on her warily as though he expected her to attack him at any moment.

Her body still burned painfully with the need to either mount or have Hunter mount her, and only the horror of the situation prevented her mind from giving over to instinct again.

"Hurry!" she said urgently. "I don't know how much longer I can stay myself!"

Hunter nodded and dashed over to the driver's side while she climbed up onto the passenger seat. She concentrated on shutting the door and buckling her seatbelt, using those simple tasks as an anchor to her sanity. The heat within was a million times worse than the worst fever she had ever had. Hell, just shifting her thighs had her groin throbbing almost unbearably with need. She clenched them together with a quiet groan. A few more minutes and Kylie was afraid she wouldn't be able to keep herself from masturbating in front of Hunter for even just a little relief.

"Hurry!" Kylie repeated pleadingly through gritted teeth, her eyes closed against seeing the living temptation beside her. Her hands clutched the seatbelt across her chest so tightly that her hands were beginning to hurt.

The truck's tires screeched horribly as Hunter peeled out from the curb. She heard several cars honking angrily at them, but Kylie was feeling so miserable that she couldn't even drum up the energy to worry about wrecking. She distracted herself by thinking about what she would do once they arrived wherever Hunter was taking her.

First and foremost, she would jump into the shower turned up to the iciest setting possible. She didn't care if she died of hypothermia. Anything would be better than the burning she was currently enduring. If this was what a female jaguar shifter endured every time they went into heat, Kylie didn't know how they managed without going insane.

"Almost there. Hang in there," Hunter abruptly said, his deep voice reverberating directly through her loins, making Kylie clench her thighs together more tightly with a moan of frustrated agony.

She heard Hunter hiss and wondered if she had accidentally bombarded him with a fresh new pheromone wave of doom. Dammit! Why didn't anyone warn her about this? She had no memories of her mother ever going through something like this!

By the time the truck stopped and she heard Hunter open the door, Kylie was practically writhing on the seat. Her eyes flew open, and not waiting for Hunter's instruction, she all but flew out of the truck. They were in a parking garage she had never seen before. The unfamiliarity of it stopped her in her tracks. She had expected Hunter to drive her to her apartment and thought she could just make a dash for her unit.

Kylie wrapped her arms around her trembling body just as Hunter cautiously walked up to her. "Follow me, but whatever you do, don't touch me. I'll make sure you get into the new apartment I've arranged for you, but for God's sake, don't even think about leaving it until your heat ends. I'll try to find a woman from our clan to come sit with you. She'll be able to explain what's going on with you better than I ever could."

"How long does a jaguar's heat last?" Kylie asked as she followed him into the building, making sure to fix her eyes on his feet.

"Twelve days usually," he replied apologetically.

She hissed in sudden anger, making her momentarily forget about the throbbing between her legs. "There's no way in hell I can miss that much college!"

"Until you learn to control your pheromone output, you'll have to."

Kylie's growl of frustration was all jaguar. She

was so upset, she didn't realize that they had reached the elevators and Hunter had stopped to push the button. Her entire front rammed into his back, her aching nipples rubbing against the cotton of her shirt as her breasts pressed against him.

A sharp growl was her only warning before Kylie's body was suddenly whirled around and her back slammed into the elevator doors, a soft, wet mouth swallowing her gasp of shock. Then her mind blanked as relief and pleasure thundered through both her mind and body.

Somewhere in the far corners of her mind, she had a vague perception of clutching tightly at Hunter's shoulders, of Hunter's hands squeezing her ass and the two of them grinding their pelvises against each other in the most delicious friction she had ever experienced while tongues tangled and they both did their best to suck the breath completely from each other's lungs.

Then the support at her back disappeared, and both Kylie and Hunter stumbled backwards into the elevator. That abrupt movement seemed to snap Hunter out of his frenzy long enough to force himself away from Kylie.

"Kylie—you have to—we *can't*—" Hunter ground out with tremendous effort as he blindly searched for the right floor button behind him, not daring to take his eyes off a *very* annoyed Kylie.

But then Kylie cupped his cock through his jeans instead of going for his lips and Hunter's lips and hands were once again on her like a beast before she could even blink. The elevator jerked as it started to rise, causing them to fall against the back wall in a tangle of limbs.

Kylie wrapped a leg around his thigh in order to grind more easily against his swollen member, causing Hunter to bite down hard enough on her bottom lip to draw blood. The salty taste seemed to drive them both into a greater frenzy, and suddenly, kissing and rubbing her body against him wasn't nearly enough.

She reached up to grip the flap of his shirt where it opened just below his neck and yanked down hard. The sound of buttons hitting the metal walls of the elevator sounded almost preternaturally loud to her heightened senses.

Hearing the sudden *ping* of the elevator reaching the designated floor was enough for Hunter to snap out of his pheromone-induced lust and tear himself away for a second time before Kylie could even run her hands up the smooth muscles of his chest. This time he didn't even try to talk to her as he rushed out of the elevator before the doors had even slid completely open, probably figuring she would follow him—as if she could do anything else in her current state.

Hunter was fumbling with the lock when Kylie caught up to him, pouncing on him just as he managed to turn the knob. They tumbled through the door, landing in a heap onto the soft, beige carpet with Kylie on top more or less straddling his waist. Hunter's willpower had apparently run out again as his arms encircled her waist possessively and his lips met hers aggressively. The sound of ripping fabric reached her ears a second before the cool air of the apartment hit her suddenly bare back. Another hard yank, and the elastic of her bra snapped.

Hunter then rolled them until he had settled his hips between her legs. He lifted himself off her body only long enough to rip the rest of her shirt and bra off, tossing them somewhere behind her, before he buried his face between her breasts and took a long, deep whiff of her scent. It was an action her jaguar side found extremely arousing.

He reached up a hand to pinch and fondle one of her breasts before moving to take the hardened nipple of the other into his mouth. Kylie moaned and arched up into that warm, wet suction, the fingers of one hand clutching a handful of his thick black locks while the other had slipped beneath the collar of his opened shirt and was in the process of digging her nails deeply into the firm muscles of his back just below his shoulder.

However, her sex continued to throb with need, and Kylie bucked her hips, trying to regain the fantastic friction she had experienced in the elevator earlier. An answering thrust of Hunter's hips had her murmuring in encouragement. God, she had never wanted another man as much as she wanted Hunter. She had to feel him thrusting inside her *now*!

"Hunter—*please*," Kylie begged, thrusting up against his hardness desperately as he continued to roughly suck and lathe attention on her nipples. "Need...inside me now...!"

She could feel Hunter's entire body tense against her, and her body tightened in anticipation. Then the warmth and weight of Hunter's body was just— gone.

Kylie's eyes flew open in enough time to see Hunter scrambling away from her across the carpet on his butt, the expression on his face a strange mixture of lust and guilt.

"I'm s-sorry!" he rasped, climbing onto his feet with the look of a man who was in agony.

He stumbled over to the door, his body trembling and jerking as though he had to fight through an invisible barrier for every step. His hand reached clumsily for the door as he staggered across the threshold.

"I'll send someone to help you, I promise!" he called in a strangled voice, as if even that had been agony, before slamming the door shut so hard that the walls shook.

Plunged into sudden darkness, Kylie lay on the floor, half-naked and so sexually frustrated that she felt as though she was about to explode from it. There was now only one real option left to her that didn't include pleasuring herself until she was raw, and she shuddered at the thought of the ice shower waiting for her as she forced herself to her feet—even as she was grateful that Hunter had been strong enough to even give her the option.

Hunter...

Kylie groaned and wondered how they could be anything but awkward the next time they saw each other. Somehow, she didn't think this desperate feeling of wanting him would go away so easily after the twelve days were up.

ABOUT THE AUTHOR

Cristina Rayne is a *New York Times* and *USA Today* bestselling author who lives in West Texas with her crazy cat and about a dozen bookcases full of fantasy worlds and steamy romances. She has a degree in Computer Science which totally qualifies her to write romances. As Fantasy is her first love, she feels if she can inject a little love into the fantastical, along with a few steamy scenes, then all the better. She is also the author of the *Claimed by the Elven King* and *Erotic Tales from the Vampire Underground* series.

TEMPTED BY THE JAGUAR #2: REVELATION

After dealing with the aftermath of her uncontrollable heat and finding a severely wounded wolf shifter within Hunter's forest territory, Kylie is put in a dangerous position where she must choose between saving two lives and revealing her secret to the worst possible person.